Lewa's

Birds

This is a work of fiction. A similarity to events, organizations, or persons, living or dead, is coincidental. The story takes place in a rural area near Vancouver, British Columbia, which of course, exists, as do other cities mentioned. However, none of the characters, or birds, have real life counterparts. The farm and village are amalgamations of any number of such places in the Fraser Valley. I wish it were otherwise, but, as of this publication, no such organization as Tropic Watch exists either, although there are many other such groups who do their best to make the lives of captive exotic birds better.

Edited by Lynne Melcombe,
www.lynnemelcombe.com

Copyright © 2022 by Rosemary Rigsby

ISBN 978-0-9939361-3-5

Also by Rosemary Rigsby

Prairie Seas, Mountain Harvest
My teacher, her life, her legacy.
Biography

I Was There. The Battle of Culloden 1746
In: War, A Collection of Poetry and Prose,
compiled by Robin Barratt
Memoir

The Ghost in Cabin 5
In: Seasons, A Collection of Poetry and Prose,
compiled by Robin Barratt
Short Fiction

Five Nights in a Turtle
Not Your Ordinary Hawaiian Vacation
Travel Memoir

Christmas Canter
In: Chicken Soup for the Soul
The Wonder of Christmas
Memoir

A Legacy of Ghosts
Novel

**For Ella, Liam (Jasper),
Caroline, and Patrick**

Who already understand.

Prologue

Rough bumping rouses her from sleep, but her head buzzes and her body aches. Blackness presses around her. She tries to open her beak, but it's shut tight. She stretches, but her wings are clamped close. She hears frantic clawing and muffled shrieks. Others are near, and like her, packed in something dark and smelly that flaps as they jolt up and down.

Branches and leaves swish overhead–the only sound at all familiar in this black terror. It hurts to breathe the cold air, and she can't fluff her feathers. Her mouth is dry, and one eye throbs.

Struggle is useless and she rests. Later, the jolting, along with human panting becomes faster. She hears shouts. Branches break and feet thud the earth. She senses that she is falling and comes to a jarring stop upside down. She rasps a call, but nobody answers. The voices come closer.

"Here, Lewa, he dropped the bag." A deep terrifying voice, and a strange zipping noise. "All in pipes, two, four–seven."

She is lifted and turned upwards. She shuts her eyes against the sudden light. She feels ill and dizzy.

"Oh no, Carlos…this is horrible." A lighter voice. "This wasn't supposed to happen. We should have stopped him sooner. Hyacinth macaws, such a loss, they are all dead."

Gentle hands pull her out of the pipe and remove the tape on her beak.

"Not all, this one is alive. Barely. It has a nasty cut."

"Agua, Carlos. Just a little. There, careful now. I'll tuck her under my shirt. She might have a chance."

Lewa's Birds

Day 1 Saturday: Alexis
Birdwatching VS Gravity

I kick the off-switch on the vacuum and lean over the table to stare, for the hundredth time, at the magazine picture of a hyacinth macaw. It perches, wings spread and beak shining, on a woman's arm. The woman has her back to the photographer. '*According to* Tropic Watch*, this is a**nother species in peril from smugglers and habitat destruction*,' reads the caption. Such an awesome bird.

Flip squawks. She watches me from her cage and blinks bright eyes.

"Yes, you're awesome too, for a cockatiel. And very cute."

I roll up the magazine and stuff it in my backpack, where my camera, in its case, waits in the bottom. Even though she's at work, my mother is in my head: *Alexis, make sure you use the case. I can't replace that camera.* I would rather have a phone, but the camera is a good digital, and reminds me that I have things to do, aside from the rest of my Saturday chores.

At the back door, I almost make it outside, but Flip screeches. She isn't about to let me go without the last word. It sounds like a question. It's in cockatiel, but sounds like: '*What's with the crumbs and fluff on the floor? And what about my house?*'

Flip hangs on the side of her smelly cage and looks at me with her crest flat. I meant to start my jobs earlier but sat reading long after Mum left for work. I drop my backpack and close the door.

"I'm sorry, you're right." I open Flip's door and she steps onto my finger. I scratch her neck. She sits on my shoulder while I clean. I stuff liner in the garbage and wrinkle my nose. I pick up the vacuum and push the nozzle under and around Flip's cage. Amazing how much mess one little bird can make.

But today of all days, I need to get to the stable. If I'd started earlier, like I hear often, I'd be done, but just once I would love a whole Saturday to do what I like.

From the basket under her cage, I pick a toy for Flip, one she hasn't had for a while. I kiss the top of her head and pop her in, hoping the toy will keep her busy for the day. She inspects the string of corks and plastic spoons and murmurs a deep throated chir-rup. Again she reminds me of my mother, who I envision talking to somebody on the phone while three other people, all holding dogs or cats, ask her questions. It's a busy clinic.

Our phone rings when I again open the door. I'll never get out of here.

"Hi, Honey. You're going to the stable today, right?"

"Just leaving now." I hear the other line ringing in the background, and somebody shouting, "Dawn!"

"Good, wear your helmet!"

I feel like shouting, *I always wear my helmet. And if I don't, it's my life*. Instead, I mumble, "Yeah, I will," but thinking *I'm fifteen, not five*.

"Gotta go. It's nutso here today."

She didn't ask about vacuuming. I'll do the rest this afternoon before she gets home. Unchaining my bike I hear, '*Doing a few chores on Saturday, so that we can do something* fun *on Sunday,*' her word for it, '*Isn't much to ask, is it Alexis?*'

It isn't too much to ask, but today's photo subject is almost finished her weekly riding lesson. I pedal along quiet streets, cross the highway, and onto a country road. The scent of mown hay tickles my nose. I watch for birds and count all I spot: robins, a hawk on the telephone pole, red-winged blackbirds in the bullrushes lining the ditch, and dozens of sparrows flying out of the willows. I speed past a field of geese but look up to see, wow, an eagle drifting along like a kite, which is why I don't pay much attention to the black pick-up parked on the side of the road. Or the door opening in front of me.

Wham!

I go over, bum first with elbows close seconds, and other bits spraddling in no particular order, backpack underneath, and my bike on top. I look up at the sky at the eagle who is probably having an eagle sized laugh.

My camera!

"Dios mío! Young lady, I am so sorry, are you okay? I did not see you coming."

A man's deep voice. *Well I'm glad he didn't do it on purpose*. I roll over, push myself onto my knees, and look up at dark grey slacks, a blue shirt with rolled up sleeves, and a slim black tie hanging off centre. Binoculars on a strap around his neck. Broad knuckles on the hand reaching down. I don't take his hand and get to my feet on my own.

"I'm fine, really. I wasn't looking either." I pull my camera out of my backpack.

"One doesn't see many cameras like that," he says.

I turn it on and off. Check the lens. It's okay. "I know. It's a good one." I look at my hand and pick out grit. I look at my elbow as if I can see through denim. I'm sure it's scraped. I will have a few bruises too. It could have been worse. I braked at the last second. I'm an idiot. I should have watched the truck. But I thought it was Maxine's. *Except, Alexis, it wouldn't be parked out here on the road.*

The man lifts my bike. He holds it with two hands, and I look up at his face. Not young, not old. Dark hair. He looks at me, and his expression shifts. Is he worried I might cry? He looks down at the bike.

"I think your bicycle has no damage." He leans over it, bounces it on its tires, and rolls it back and forth. It's second-hand too and was hardly in great condition when Mum bought it. But again, not easy to replace.

He holds my bike with one hand. With the other, he pushes back strands of hair. Dark deep-set eyes flick from me to the bike and to where the lane to the stable slopes up from the road. As if mesmerized, I follow his flicking eyes and see a dark blue van parked at the back door of the stable. I frown. Nobody parks there. The man's eyes follow my gaze.

"You sure you are okay? Maybe I call your mother? Her name?" He reaches to a pocket.

"Dawn. But she's at work." I tuck my camera away.

"Dawn?"

I shoulder my backpack, looking up to see his eyebrows go back to normal. "Dawn. A lovely name. I can drive you home." He nods to the pick-up but pushes my bike toward me.

"No, thanks, I'm okay. I just need to get to the stable."

"Ah," he says, looking there as if it suddenly rose out of the ground. "A fine old building, is it not? Have you been inside?"

"Uh, well, yes…I work there, just not today. And I ride there. Sometimes. If we have money." I look at my hands on the grips. "The horse I ride is there, that is. I don't ride *in* the stable." *Man, did I hit my head?*

"Of course. So only horses in the stable then?" He shifts as he speaks, and the black eyes stare into mine.

"Yes, only horses. It's a riding stable. The Hosford-Lees own it. For people who ride in jumping shows and such, or for people who want to take lessons or board their horses. No cows or other farm animals. Say, I have to go."

"Good day then, young lady." He bows slightly, and I push off on my bike, the hair on my arms standing up.

R. Rigsby

Day 1 Saturday: Alexis
Lofty Ambitions

I pedal up the lane pushing hard on the gravel slope. Beyond the far end of stable, in the big ring, Janey on Pinball and two other riders canter around the outside. Maxine calls instructions. Janey spots me and raises her crop in a gloved hand. I dip my head at her.

"*Miss* Perrault," if you would be so kind as to give this lesson your full attention." Maxine is being sarcastic, but she never calls me *Miss* Jensen.

Horses in the paddocks swivel ears at me, hoping for a treat. Ace and Firefly, Toady and Fancy, grey and brown, chestnut and roan. I have favourites, but I don't stop to hand out wilted carrots. I look straight ahead at the stable. It really is a fine old building, as the man said. Cait says the stable is close to one hundred years old. Mitch said so. It houses horses, but it wouldn't matter if it was home to pigs or goats or tractors. Ever since Mum brought me here to play with Cait when she visited Maxine, Cait and I begged to go into the stable.

It's as tall as a four-story house. A row of windows near the eaves reflects the sun. They're not centred on the wall, as if another window should be at the end. I love the wide timber siding and the sloped angles of the roof. Cait said the only changes are the bathroom addition and repairs on this end.

Where that van is parked. Make that dirty blue van with 'Mitsubishi' on a large plate on the front. I've never seen it before and, wow, that's different–the steering wheel is on the right. Huh. The Hosford-Lees have a red car and the black pick-up, and Mitch drives a brown rust-bucket hatchback. All visitors are supposed to park in front of the riding ring on the far side of the stable, so why is this person so special?

* * *

Janey pulls Pinball to a halt. His brown and white sides heave. He paws the ground and stretches his neck. Janey releases the reins and takes her feet out of the stirrups, long legs dangling. She takes off her helmet and shakes out her hair. "Lex, you're so anal," she laughs.

"Jas gets loads of pictures; these have to be exceptional." I stand up from where I kneeled in the mulch and scroll through pictures.

"You should have been here an hour ago."

"I know. I had to clean Flip's cage." Not entirely true. I haven't told Janey about the strange incident on the road.

"And I'm not that crazy to see my face in the school newsletter thing. Nothing newsworthy about me."

"Everybody says that. Uh, that is they say they don't think *they* are newsworthy, not that *you* aren't. I look up from my camera. I have some good shots, but...the stable's loft door is open. "I'm going up there." I climb the fence, drop to my feet on the other side, and head to the stable doors. "Besides, I like taking pictures."

"I know, I shouldn't bug you. One day you'll be a famous photographer. You must have thousands of pictures!" I hear the smile in Janey's voice. "Hurry up if you want a ride. Pinny thinks it's time to quit, and I'm leaving early."

Janey's voice fades as I walk on thick plank floors, thinking about her profile and pictures for the paper, the last of the year. I want them to be the best yet. Because Jas asked me, and maybe, because well I'm sure Royce doesn't check every page for my shots.

I run my hand along the black iron grillwork that tops the box stalls. Thick beams cross overhead. People have carved initials, horse shapes, and names of long-gone horses into some of the beams, and, wow, there's a parrot! It doesn't look recent, but I never noticed it before.

Up ahead, Mitch backs out of a stall. He rubs Ace's head as pulls the door shut and slides the bolt. I want to get into the loft without him seeing me. I'm not working so I shouldn't go up there. Something to do with insurance, Cait said. I really want that shot. I step into an empty stall thinking Mitch will go down the aisle to the back door.

He does, but there's no escaping Brillo, Mitch's personal alarm system. Terrier-cross. More like cross terrier. She growls and yaps. I step out of the stall and walk as if I always detour through empty stalls.

"Oh, it's you." Mitch pokes his cap farther back on his head and scratches his forehead. "You're not working today, are you?"

I freeze in mid-step, straighten and turn to look into cool hazel eyes. "Ah, no, n-n-not working today.

Tomorrow." I wish I could answer Mitch without stammering. I lift my camera. "N-n-no, just going up to the loft to get a good shot of Janey and Pinball–for the school paper–just want–an unusual angle..." I look at my Nikes."

"Hmm. Well then, sure, go for it. Straight up, straight down, right?"

Mitch is already three steps away when I look up from my feet. Brillo, following her God, looks over her shoulder with one lip curled.

A few stalls down, I hear a sneeze. A forkful of dirty straw thumps into the wheelbarrow. Cait looks up and wipes her nose on her sleeve.

"Where are you going?"

"To the loft to take more pictures of Janey."

"Oh. Okay." I wonder at the odd tone and expect a warning about not falling down the stairs and causing an insurance claim. She hesitates, but then "On your way by, tell that horse of mine what I go through to keep her fed." She sneezes again.

"Oh Cait, June is awful for you. Or is it just the fresh hay in here?"

"I don't know. It's supposed to be a mild hay allergy, but yeah, could be extra stuff in the air."

I nod, walk on, then back up. "Whose van is outside?"

Her expression changes from her usual grin-and-get-on-with-it-sneezes-and-all to a frown.

"Oh, maybe a client. I'll tell Uncle Mitch–maybe they don't know to park in front."

Uncle Mitch? She never calls him that. Yeah, he is her uncle, but, I think a second, he's only twenty-five. Maxine's younger brother. Cait only calls him *uncle* when she's being funny. She turns back to raking the stall.

R. Rigsby

Day 1 Saturday: Alexis
The Lady in the Loft

I pass the tack-room and give Firefly a dutiful pat before I run up the broad stairs near the back door. I don't bother with the light because I can easily see where the stairwell ends on a square landing that is walled and roofed like a little room. It keeps loose hay from drifting down the steps to the aisle below.

I cross the landing and push the door on the far side. Bales of fresh hay rise in pale green tiers to the next set of crossbeams high above my head. I've been up these stairs dozens of times since Mitch hired me, but I never tire of the high airy space and the scent of fresh hay. Poor Cait! But she never complains and only takes a pill when she absolutely can't breathe. The bright square of light overlooking the riding ring makes me blink.

Between the stable wall and the bales, I pass a row of chutes on my right. Each one leads to a manger in a stall below. There's another row for the stalls on the other side. I pad through loose hay. Hopeful nickers echo in the chutes and repeat from somewhere above the rafters.

"So sorry, not on the job, and it's not dinner time yet." I pestered Maxine for a year about working here, but Maxine, although she owns the place and is supposedly my mother's good friend, insisted that hiring stable staff was Mitch's job, and if I wanted to work, I better work on him. My nagging finally paid off, and I started in March when I turned fifteen. Every Sunday, I clean stalls, sweep the aisles, and feed horses.

At the loft door, I look down at Janey on Pinball. She leans forward and strokes his neck. Her dad is a dentist, oh right, not just a dentist, an *orthodontist*, and her mother works for a charity. Her brother, Royce, plays hockey, and Janey has Pinball. Cait, like me, is kind of fatherless too–her dad, Bill Lee, plays in a band and he's often out on tour. Like now. At least she knows where he is and talks to him every day.

My father is some guy my mother never mentions, but she didn't find me under a cabbage leaf. Like me, she is also Miss Jensen. There isn't and never has been a Mr. Anybody with us. The only other relatives we have are my mother's Auntie Beth and Uncle Nick.

Uncle Nick stands in when we celebrate Father's Day which is two weeks away and never that big of a deal. Janey's dad came from a prairie farm and had horses, so I guess Janey's horse-bug is inherited. I think he played hockey too. I have no idea what I inherited, but keeping a horse is big money and a lot of work, and I have Flip. I pick a bale and sit in front of the loft door.

"Are you ever going to take this picture?" Janey, feet back in stirrups, but blond hair loose on her shoulders, trots Pinball in a circle. She laughs. "If you want to have a ride before Maxine needs the ring again, you better hurry up! Dad will be here any second."

I click away ten or twelve times, hoping that one will be the ultimate shot. With her huge smile, and flowing hair, Janey looks like Lady Godiva before she got the bright idea to ride naked, or maybe an equestrienne Lady Gaga. I give her a thumbs-up before I brush hay off my jeans and trot back to the landing.

Pulling the door open, I see two feet, rather two lace-up leather boots right in front of my face. My heart leaps into my throat, but the boots aren't swinging. They're on a ladder against the wall beside the door. I look up to see the boots are followed by a long floral skirt, a beaded and crocheted (I think) jacket, and a face peering down at me over a shoulder swathed in a loose reddish scarf or shawl. Her head is just below a rectangular hole in the ceiling of the landing.

Without thinking, I say, "Whhho are you?" Heat rushes to my face. So rude. And the babyish stammering is worse. After all, she might be Maxine's friend. Or Mitch's? But why would she be here, or rather up there? "I'm sorry, I, I mean – ah…" and can't finish. Is there another floor up there?

In answer to my question, the face, backdropped in the light, with a mass of curling hair that is some shade of grey, light brown, or blond, says, "Lewa."

R. Rigsby

Day 1 Saturday: Lewa
The Inevitable

Now of all the people I don't want to see, that girl is right under my feet when I come down from the loft. I see her eyes and nearly fall off the ladder. Why do I tell her my name? I'm getting soft.

"Bloody Hell," I mutter as I watch her practically run down the stairs. Maxine told me the girl would be around but said she would watch her friend do her lesson, hang out with the horse, and then go home. Today, of all days, she decides to wander around the loft?

I should have been more careful, but while scrubbing the windows, I saw a black ute parked by the road. I wanted to get a closer look, because if Carlos didn't go looking me in Montreal, he would come here.

I'll bet a Tim-Tam to a pink possum he's found me and sooner than I hoped. Thousands of kilometres of dirt can't disguise my van. If it was him. I hear that girl running to the other end of the stable, so I go downstairs and look out the door. No ute. Maybe I'm overreacting. I hear Mitch in the feed-room having a conversation with his dog and the barn cat.

"You need to get a life, Mitch."

He looks up and turns pink. "If it isn't my long-lost cousin! Make that never-mentioned cousin. I thought you were a myth."

"Like the Loch Ness monster?" I laugh, and he does too. "Nothing mythical about me. Good to see you again. You've grown since I saw you last."

"I just remember your hair. But, yeah, glad to meet you. I think. I got in late last night and Max only gave me the Cole's Notes version of why you're here. She said something about delivering a parrot."

"A macaw for the conservatory, but just before Kamloops they called to say they couldn't take it yet."

"Cait said she thought her mother would keel over when you came in the door. Why didn't we know you were coming?"

"Van kept stalling, then my phone went flat. Once I got the van going, I couldn't stop to recharge. I had a suite booked in the village, but I can't keep two birds there. My bird is quiet for a parrot, but the other bird can shriek. I asked Maxine if I could leave one in her house."

"Cait said she sneezed as soon as you opened the van, and the squawking was unbelievable."

"They were fed up with being stuck in crates. I expected Maxine to tell me to move on, but she said we could open the loft room. I was surprised the cages were still there. And a good thing because the crates are disgusting."

I step into the feed-room doorway and look out the back door toward the road. "Did you see a black ute, er, truck, parked on the road?"

"I saw a dark pick-up go by when I brought in a horse, but nothing parked. Lots of such trucks out here. Why?"

"You remember Carlos?"

"Nope, I was ten when I saw you last, and don't remember any friends of yours. Did you know him before you, ah–"

"Yes. We worked together then, as we do now, but we've had a difference of opinion. He wants to…talk to me."

"So, a bit of a tiff going on?" Mitch grins and pushes back his cap. "Does he have something to do with your interest in black trucks?"

"Probably doesn't matter. And that girl was in the loft. She saw me."

"Max said you would be up there all day. The kid just wanted to take a few pictures. She's still here–out in the lesson ring with her friend. Max didn't say why it matters." Mitch raises an eyebrow but shakes out a sack of oats and closes the bin. "I know a little of what happened years ago, but not everything. Not exactly part of Hosford clan lore."

"No, I guess I don't figure in family stories over coffee and cake. I'll tell you more tomorrow when I come back. Won't be till after six when your horse people are gone. I'll finish upstairs, then go buy parrot feed."

Later, and with another glance at the empty road, I open Mitzi's door. Silly to name a van, but it fits. The bloke out there might have stopped to take pictures of the geese or talk on his phone or blow his nose. My grand plan can still work, even with the hiccup that brings me here. I hold my breath, but Mitzi starts right away. I should apologize to Mitch. It's not his fault I almost jumped on top of the girl.

Alexis, Maxine said. Things could get prickly if the little madam asks questions about me. On top of everything else, the last thing I need is a confrontation with Dawn. Or Beth and Nick.

Day 2 Sunday: Alexis
Lewa's Ladder

Janey peeks through the iron grill between Pinball's stall and the one I'm mucking out. "*Lewa*? That's really her name?" She screws up her face and hangs on to a bar on either side of that face. Like she's in jail.

"That's what she said. Lewa. Her name is Lewa." I heave a pitchfork full of straw and manure into the wheelbarrow in the aisle.

"And she came down from above the loft. Do you know what's up there? What was she doing?"

"Yes. No. I don't know." I prop the fork on top of my load and stand up straight to stretch. Minou twines around my legs and rubs her face on my jeans. She lifts each front foot, kneading the bits of straw on the wooden floor. I lean down and stroke her tabby back. Pinny lowers his head and heaves a big horse sigh. For once, Janey is stuck for words. She picks up a section of brown and white tail and stares at it. This was my first chance to tell her about Lewa.

* * *

Yesterday, once I recovered my brains at seeing a person dressed in such a weird outfit clinging to a ladder I never noticed, I thumped down the stairs, and ran into the ring to get my ride on Pinball. Janey threw me the reins, then dashed into the stable to grab her coat just as her father pulled up.

"Lucky me–dentist," she called as she got in.

Just a regular dentist, not an *orthodondist*. Pinball and I trotted, cantered, and then walked until he was cool. I brushed him and gave him a wrinkled apple I found in the bottom of my backpack. Then I biked home.

Mum's car was in the carport, and I thought I was dead. She should have been at work. When I went in, I heard her say goodbye and something about talking more later before hanging up the phone. Her face was set, but the mouth part smiled at me.

I didn't ask who was on the phone or why she was home early. Nope, I went straight for the vacuum cleaner. She didn't say a word. When I finished, we went to Auntie Beth's for dinner, where I was the best nicey nicey kid ever. While I washed lettuce, Mum, Auntie, and Uncle Nick had their heads together in the living room. At home, I kissed Mum goodnight and went to bed.

* * *

I step over Minou and shove the wheelbarrow to a short passage between two stalls about halfway down the aisle. A doorway at the end opens onto a raised plank gangway that leads to the manure pile. Grunting, I upend dung and dirty straw onto the heap.

I trundle back with the wheelbarrow, puffing like a big bad wolf. Mitch said I was too small for the job but let me go on trial for a month. I passed.

"Did you see her again before you left?" Janey calls.

"No. I saw the blue van leave and I guessed it was hers. I brushed Pinball and put the tack away and left right after cuz Mum and I were having dinner at our aunt and uncle's."

I dodged a bullet for not doing the rest of my chores. I think that the odd look on Mum's face had something to do with it. I have no idea what that was about. Was she guilty about leaving work early? She never did say why she was home.

In the next stall, I fork more poop and smelly straw into the wheelbarrow.

"I told Auntie Beth about Lewa and the loft though, when she came to help me with the salad, and Mum stayed in the living room with Uncle Nick."

"Lex, what did your aunt say?"

"Nothing. She looked surprised for a moment but didn't ask questions."

"She didn't say '*Lewa who*?' Does your aunt know Lewa?"

"I don't know, but she used to ride here ages ago, and she's friends with Cait's Gramma and Gramp. Has been forever. Then she said it was time to eat, and I didn't ask again." There was something weird about the conversation during dinner, or rather the lack of it, and every time I opened my mouth to ask about Lewa, I closed it.

Janey coos nonsense into Pinball's ears, then peers around the edge of the stall at me. "Shouldn't Mitch or Cait know her? Where are they?"

"Mitch took Cait and Firefly to a riding clinic." And I probably won't ask Mitch about Lewa. So grumpy lately. I rumble the next load to the manure dump. From the ramp I see a dark blue SUV coming up the drive–the Perrault clan come to collect Janey for dinner with her grandmother. Her mother's mother who's come for a visit. Janey has a full set of grandparents in Saskatchewan. I have none. They were killed in a crash when my mother was little.

I wait on the ramp and shade my eyes as I watch the Perrault SUV. Royce has both hands on the wheel and looks straight up the lane. His dad sits beside him with his elbow on the edge of the open window. From the back seat, Janey's mother waves as the car rounds the far end of the stable.

I upend my load and push the wheelbarrow down the aisle, pitchfork rattling. Royce stands outside Pinball's stall and watches me. If I laid my face on a bale, my cheeks would start a fire. I'm grubby and sweaty. He wears dark-wash jeans and a white t-shirt. *White*? I can't wear anything white for two minutes without getting it mucked up. Tall, like Janey, he smiles at me from under dark blond hair. Grey-green eyes, like Janey, and like her, he smiles and laughs a lot.

I'm a brown bird. A scruffy brown bird who can barely cheep. I smile, although most of my hair has escaped the elastic and headband and hangs in my face. I reposition the purple headband. It doesn't do a great job and tends to slip off.

"Hi Lex! How's it going? Has my sister let you ride her nag?" Royce rubs Pinball's nose. Pinball snuffs and nudges his arm.

Janey, on her way to the tack-room with her caddy of brushes and picks, calls back. "I sure have.

She spends almost as much time looking after him as I do."

Royce grins at me and offers Pinball the small apple he held behind his back. "Janey says the school paper will be the best yet because you're doing her profile and pictures."

"She says no such thing. She doesn't even want to be in it. I mean, she's okay with the profile, but I'm not a real photographer…"

"Well you're just a kid…" It's Royce's turn to lose the words. "…but your pictures are great." We're saved by a beeping horn.

"Hurry up Lame-Jane, Dad must be starving."

"Are you driving?" Janey gives Pinball a final pat and closes his door.

"Yup! Get my real license next week."

"You mean you get to take the test; don't be so sure you'll pass…Bye Lex."

More banter drifts back as they shove each other out the door. Royce says he had lots of practice last summer at the farm. Janey says big deal even she can drive a tractor. I lean on my pitchfork and put my chin on my arm.

An hour later, I prop the wheelbarrow in the feed-room and hang the shovel and fork. I sit on an overturned bucket and pull my water bottle from my backpack. Gulping large mouthfuls, I rub my other grimy hand on my jeans. Minou purrs on a saddle pad. Outside in the ring, Maxine calls instructions to four riders jumping a pattern of low fences. *Ms. Hosford, would you be so kind as to speak up*, I choke on the last slurp. I could ask Maxine about Lewa, but she makes me stammer even more than Mitch.

Other horse people tack up, or brush, or lead their mounts in and out. Horse nickers and talking people offset the booming of shod feet on dense planks. I inhale the aroma of hay and grain, warm horseflesh, and the earthy scent of horse buns. I sigh. Mum is picking me up today, and I should get cleaned up. Normally I throw the shovel and fork at the wall and rush out to watch the lessons, but not today. I drop my water bottle on my backpack and stand up.

I stop a few steps up the loft stairs. Nothing stirs, and nobody is up above. Cait and Mitch haven't come back, and the blue van isn't parked at the back door. Feeding, my last task of the day, can wait a few minutes.

I look up the dim stairwell. I step up two more stairs. Below, the muffled sounds of people and horses, sounding farther away than they really are. Up here, quiet. I look up at the landing. I wouldn't be surprised if there was no ladder. Wouldn't be surprised if I imagined meeting Lewa. After all, I was in a hurry for my ride, and I often have dreams…but I was neither sleeping nor daydreaming, was I?

I can just make out the ladder. I walk up and look to where it goes through the hole in the ceiling of the landing. At the roof. The ladder leads nowhere.

Day 2 Sunday: Alexis
To a Mystery Door

The hair on my neck lifts and my stomach goes hollow. I imagined it. But Lewa…who can dream up a name like that? She was real–she spoke, and now I think about it, she smelled. Okay, not a *smell* smell, but she had an aroma that reminded me of something.

My hair lays back down. *Oh, really Alexis?* Again, I look up through the hole in the landing's ceiling. The high roof of the stable soars into darkness. From this angle I can't see the huge crossbeams that sweep across the loft and support the roof. Shafts of light leak through shrunken siding and dust whirls in the glow.

The bottom of the ladder is above the top of my head which is why I probably never noticed it before. It's doubled-up and hooked. No harm in seeing where it goes. I unhook it and pull it down. It thumps the floor. I jump and look down the stairs. How would I explain this to Mitch? I step on the first rung, knowing every step will be harder to explain. If I shouldn't be here. Why shouldn't I be here?

Once above the room's ceiling, I look over my shoulder and am surprised to see several pet carriers covered in dust. Each would hold a medium sized dog. Was this what Lewa was doing? But what an odd, and awkward, place to store anything. My eyes adjust to the light as I look out over the loft. On the north end, overlooking the ring, the big double door is closed today. Bales of hay form an elongated pyramid as high as my line of sight and extend all the way into darkness at the other end of the stable.

The ladder continues up the wall to a narrow platform. From there a catwalk leads to the dark end where I can just make out a door. A door? I haul myself up. The planks of the catwalk are barely the width of my two feet.

"Only Minou can do this well." I clench my teeth and grip the narrow rail on the open side. It's sturdy, but I don't want to test it. I don't look down, one hand on the rail, and the other feeling along the wall to the door. It must enter this walled-off level above the stack of hay. I never noticed that before either. On a hook hangs what looks like a shoulder harness with straps and snaps. What the heck is this for? Maxine's voice, blurred by distance reminds me where I am. From below comes the muffled chatter of people and snorts and nickers of horses. Nickers come from beyond the door. Is there a horse in there? *That really is ridiculous, Alexis.*

I grip the tarnished doorknob and give it a quarter turn. The stable breathes around me. Drafts sigh past my face, bearing the aromas of a barn in the country: sweet hay, sour manure, dust, and animals, and something else.

I sniff. There's that smell again and I think of Lewa. Does she live up here? I snatch my hand away as if the knob might burst into flame. I'm trespassing, and if somebody thought it my business to climb up to this door, they would have told me about it.

When Mitch hired me, Cait showed me how to cut the binder twine, and separate the flakes of hay from the bales, and how much to give to each horse. I had to remember which chute led to which stall, and if I couldn't remember how many flakes a certain horse received, I was to go back down the stairs and look at the notes on the whiteboard. Easy.

She didn't say, "Hey look up and see that catwalk? See the door at the other end of the loft? Any time you like just take yourself on a stroll up there and check it out. It's totally okay."

And neither Cait nor Mitch mentioned Lewa. Not a word. And Lewa when I stammered my rude, *Who are you,* only said her name. At which I muttered *sorry*, lifted my camera and then took off down the stairs. I didn't wait to see if Lewa followed, or went back up the ladder, or disappeared into thin air.

That's silly. Nobody disappears. Lewa has that van. She's real. And so is this door. I push my hair back.

Bang!

And so is that door somewhere below. Lessons are over and people and horses bump around in the stalls and aisles. Some horses stamp. Before an impatient owner comes up in search of their horse's dinner, I scuttle along the catwalk and back down the ladder. I pull apart a bale and flakes of number one alfalfa fall into mangers and the mouths of hungry horses. What's in the secret room?

I drop hay into the last chute and my mother's voice wafts from below. Halfway down the stairs, remembering the ladder, I turn back and re-hook it. Mum's chatting with Maxine outside the tack-room.

"Yes, we're going to eat out, and see a show, which is why I'm here picking her up."

"Dawn. When are you going to say something?" Maxine says. "You know it's time. Way beyond time."

I stop and listen. Say something to who?

"I know, I know, but Uncle Nick wants to be sure she's ready and then just get on with the inevitable."

Oh, that's it. Mum wants them to move to a condo. The house is too much work for them.

"And there's something else," says Maxine, but I clomp down the steps.

Mum pokes her head into the stairwell. "Oh, hi there, Sweetie, I wondered where you were. Have you decided where you would like to eat this evening? Are you hungry? I'll load your bike. Just come out when you're cleaned up."

I nod like a bobblehead. Not much chance of getting a word in. Maxine's cheek twitches as she half-smiles at me and follows Mum back down the aisle.

Day 2 Sunday: Lewa
As Good a Story as Any

A soft breeze sighs around the trees lining the village street where I parked my van. I spent most of the day catching up on sleep in my rental suite. My bird also was tired and is happy to rest on her standing perch and play with her string of wooden balls. I wind down Mitzi's window and clench my teeth, but Mitzi, maybe also enjoying the ambience of this little town, starts on the third go. She's spluttering more than usual again. I don't see any black trucks on the way to the stable and I park at the main door, relying on a row of tall cottonwoods to screen the view from the road.

Mitch and Cait appear in the doorway. A nice girl, Cait, but she has questions. Maxine said she doesn't need to know everything. Yet.

"We were sweeping up," Mitch says, but you have homework, don't you?" He raises his brows at Cait and takes her broom.

"I always have homework. Bye, Lewa."

I follow Mitch down the aisle. A few horses drop their heads over stall doors, and I pat noses. I like horses, but never as much as parrots. I glance up, and yes, there it is, that figure I carved so many years ago.

Mitch hangs the brooms, and in the tack-room resumes the never-ending job of cleaning saddles. I sit on a stool. He buffs a cloth back and forth over a dark leather saddle, then cocks an eyebrow at me.

May as well dive in. "What do you remember from when you saw me last?"

"The ruckus after they carted you away. Everybody shouting at each other. Nick trying to referee. Was Carlos there?"

"No, he slithered off." I sigh. "He continued to work for Tropic Watch, and later, after my time, they took me back."

"Right. Max told me about that group. They do good work."

"Yes. But I might be sacked."

"What happened?"

"They didn't exactly give me approval to take that bird to the conservatory."

"And Carlos doesn't approve either and this isn't just a lover's spat?"

"Far from it. And I think Carlos has other problems."

"Like what?"

"I can't say for sure, but I think he's in over his head."

"Like you?"

Mitch is shrewder than I thought. I shrug. "I don't know how far in I am. But as soon as the conservatory can take that bird, I'll explain it all to my contact at Tropic Watch."

Mitch puts away the saddle, and I get off my stool.

"Maxine doesn't know, does she? You could stay here at the farm. Lots of room in the house."

"Maxine offered, but I don't want to stay here because of…"

Mitch stops in mid-reach hanging a bridle. "Shouldn't you and Dawn figure things out? It's been a long time."

"It has. But she hates me. And I don't blame her."

Mitch pinches the bridge of his nose. "Want to come up to the house when you're done upstairs? Have a coffee?"

I smile. That sounds so normal, so much like what families do together, but I shake my head. "Ta, but no, I'll stay out of Maxine's way as much as possible. When this is over, maybe."

R. Rigsby

Day 3 Monday: Alexis
Something Smells

I race-walk down the hall to the newsletter office beside Mr. Thoms' room. Something burning in the cooking lab reminds me of last night's dinner with Mum. I said I wanted a burger. They were overcooked, like Uncle Nick's victims on the barbeque, and the place was noisy. Mum questioned me on the usual stuff about friends and school but asked if I minded passing on the show since she had a headache. I said no problem because I kept thinking of Janey's profile. I used Mum's clunker of a desk-top computer to finish the write-up, copied the pictures off my camera, and emailed the whole works to Jas and Mr. Thoms.

If they aren't what they want, I'm not sure when I can try again. Janey has dance or band or debating club nearly every day after school. I cross my fingers. Mr. Thoms and Jas have their heads over a computer screen, and both look up when I hover in the doorway. Usually Jas just says yes, good enough.

"Lex! Great job on the profile and especially the pictures. Love the angles."

Mr. Thoms nods. "We're squeezing in more shots."

I nearly swallow my gum. "Oh, good, b-b-but just good luck, I guess…"

Jas frowns, and says, "Yeah whatever," and turns back to the computer screen.

I sleepwalk through lunch to the point that Janey asks me if I feel okay. I'm not, but shrug and fold up my lunch-bag. Janey can chatter non-stop to anybody about anything, or about nothing, and is never stuck for words. I become mute as soon as I hear something unexpected. When Janey is with me, she jumps in and saves me. Since kindergarten.

***

At my desk in my room supposedly doing homework, I think about my 'lack of social eloquence,' a phrase I read somewhere. Too bad I can't think of the big words in a real conversation. Even little words would do.

I doodle and open my math text. Between doodling and working an algebra equation, I turn pages in my magazine. Or rather, Uncle Nick's magazine, *Planet and Nature*, that I borrowed from him. I tried to give it back on Saturday after dinner, but he said I could keep it. I re-read the best article, one of the two-parts piece on endangered parrots and other 'bird trade' birds that are wild caught and smuggled. In the sidebar, an italicised paragraph mentions a group called Tropic Watch which is *instrumental in bird rescue and rehabilitation.*

I look again at the picture of the woman holding the hyacinth macaw, her hair bound in an orange scarf. The other pictures are macaws, red, as well as blue and gold, cockatoos from Australia, and African greys. Who wouldn't want one of these birds as a pet? But I guess that's the problem. I sigh, look at the photographs, and think of my own bird pictures.

I have hundreds of Flip and lots of herons and eagles and the other birds that live around here. Even gulls. And horses. I have selfies of me, and some shots of my friends if they let me. And some of Mum and Auntie Beth and Uncle Nick. I open my camera and look at Janey and Pinball. Farther back, there's a nice one of Royce with the track team, and a few of Cait and Firefly.

Cait and I have been friends since we were babies. Our mothers are friends, and Auntie Beth and Cait's Gramma have been friends forever. We're like cousins, but Cait is a few months older. She mostly hangs around with other grade ten kids, especially Jas. The serious Cait told me she needs the best possible grades this year and especially next year, because that's the year that really counts toward university entrance. Who looks that far ahead? I can barely figure out what I'm doing next week. I doodle a clock on the corner of the page.

Do I want to go to university too? Or at least to a college? Assuming there would be money. What do I want to do? I have no idea. Photography? I take lots of pictures, but could I make a living at it? Do I want to?

I push my pencil across the page that should be filled with completed algebra equations instead of horse heads and birds. And a clock. The horse heads look pretty much the same, but the birds: parrots, cockatiels like Flip, and cockatoos, are better.

Flip wakes from a nap, lifts and resettles her feathers, screeches, and throws stuff out of her cage. I laugh. I open her door and hold out a finger onto which she steps with immense dignity. Then she upends this dignity by hanging upside down. Her one trick, for which she is named.

She flaps herself upright. I scratch her neck and she closes her eyes, opens her beak, and leans into my fingers. Cockatiel ecstasy. I set her down in front of me. She walks up and down on my pencil, has a look at the unfinished algebra problems and doodles, and pronounces my page only worthy of the small deposit she makes in the middle of it. I laugh, then stop. I lean toward Flip's cage and take a deep whiff. There's that smell.

Did Lewa smell of bird? Or more precisely bird poop? How could that be? *Don't be silly Alexis.* Maybe she keeps birds at home. But then, why had I caught a scent of that distinctive aroma–like when Flip's cage really needs cleaning–at that door? I'll ask Cait about Lewa. If Lewa is upping and downing a ladder in the stable, and owns that van, then Cait must know who she is.

Day 4 Tuesday: Alexis
An Assignment in Anxiety

All morning between classes, I run up and down stairs to catch Cait at her locker or alone. She has lots of friends. Just before lunch, I finally flag her down. She looks at me, looks at Jas and others waiting at the end of the hall, then looks at me again.

I think she's about to sneeze, but she waves and mouths at Jas to go ahead, and then she does sneeze.

"Whew, that one snuck up on me." She laughs, smothering another sneeze.

I blurt out, "What do you know about Lewa? And that room in the loft?" She peers at me from between brown bangs and the tissue she has plastered to her face.

"Lewa. Right. My cousin, er, second cousin, I guess. She's Australian. That room used to be for stable hands years ago before my grandparents took down the outside stairs."

"Are you coming?" Jas is back.

"Lex, we'll talk about this later, okay? But do me a favour. Don't tell anybody you met Lewa." Cait trots away.

"Sure." She didn't explain a thing. Why not mention Lewa? I already told Auntie and Janey. Lewa must use the room. For what? More dog crates? Yoga?

Maybe she's a witch and conjures nickering mice. Does she do that in Australia too? Cait's grandparents are there visiting. Nobody has ever mentioned Lewa. Which is weird considering Mum and I have often joined the Hosford-Lees for dinner. Often with Auntie Beth and Uncle Nick. Are there any more mystery cousins? Shouldn't Cait say so? After all, our mothers are like sisters.

I'll catch Cait later when I'm closer to the top of her priority list. My stomach gurgles. It would like lunch. At the track, Janey said. I shade my eyes and spot her on the top bleachers with Rennie and Kendra, laughing, eating, and watching some of the track team doing laps. Royce pounds by, gaining on Aziz. He glances at me, then turns on the jets and closes the gap. I climb up, sit down, and peer into my lunch bag as if it holds a surprise. It doesn't because I make my own lunch.

"Ooooo," Kendra says to Janey, "your brother is sooo fast," and then laughs like a maniac. I want to push her over backwards, just to see all that long black hair fly through the air.

After school, a new worry edges out thoughts of Lewa and the secret room over the stable, as well as the annoying Kendra. I stare at my feet as I walk down the steps with Janey.

"Now what's with you?" she says. "You've hardly said a word since English."

"It's that assignment."

"Which one?"

"The speaking assignment from Miss Gibbs. I can't stand in front of the class and talk for five minutes. I feel sick thinking about it."

"Oh it'll be fun! We'll be videoed for the school's You-Tube channel. I'll help you. Hey look, there's Cait and Jas and Royce and Kendra. Let's catch up. They're going to the Snack Shack."

"You go. I left my camera in my locker."

"Uh, okay, you can always come and find us there." Janey calls over her shoulder as she strides down the steps.

I hardly ever fib to Janey. My camera is in my backpack, as always, but I should go to the library. I turn and go back into the school. *It'll be fun* Janey said and I guess it will be for her. What on earth am I going to talk about? If I can manage to squeak out a few words without throwing up.

I could talk about riding or horses, but Janey will likely do that, and she knows way more than me. My life is a bore. I know about shovelling muck out of stalls. I could put everybody to sleep. I could talk about my bird. But how lame is that? It's something I might have done in grade six. Nobody now wants to hear about a pet bird, no matter how cute she is.

The windowed library door is shut. I push the handle and butt my forehead on the glass. Right below a taped-up piece of paper. Locked. Several people sitting at one of the tables turn to look at me, probably wondering why I'm bonking my head on the door. On Tuesdays, the parent counsel meets in the library, per the notice above my head.

Okay, now what? Go home? But Mum won't be home for another hour, and I don't feel like hanging in my room with my bird, reading, or watching TV. Or vacuuming. The Snack Shack. I pull change out of my pocket: enough for a Coke, but nothing else. I need more hours at work. This summer maybe?

At the crosswalk, I wait for a green recycling truck to pass. I could go along the street, up two blocks and across a block, but the best way from the school to the Snack Shack is by a walkway between two condo buildings. Then it crosses an alley and continues between the pharmacy and the old hotel, now converted to apartments.

I cross the street and enter the walkway bordered by the patios and gardens of the ground floor condos. I take out my camera and focus on a pot of blossoms. Geraniums, I think. I squat and aim at the flowers in the foreground with the walkway beyond. I click away.

A flurry of motion on the other side of the alley catches my attention. I stand up to see a flash of orange, a scarf maybe, on a woman who stands in a doorway. A dark figure steps toward her, but then the recycling truck rumbles in front and stops. I wait for it to upend the bin of cardboard and when it leaves, whoever was in the walkway is gone.

I think the figure was a man. Was the woman Lewa? Why do I think so? I cross the alley and pause outside a doorway with a sign: 'Furnished Studios for Rent.' One of the curtained windows is slightly open, and I hear talking. And a squawk? A lady watering flowers watches me. I still have my camera in my hand, so I put it away and move on.

"Hey, look who came after all!" Janey jumps up and pats the seat of the booth. "Here, sit beside Royce."

Before I can drop my backpack, she's back with a stool from the counter. She perches, legs crossed, reminding me of a heron. Or a crane. If herons or cranes have blond hair, beaming smiles, and petite noses instead of beaks. I breathe, and peer from under my hair at Royce. He winks.

Kendra sits on the edge of the booth opposite me. Cait is between her and Jas who has one long arm along the window ledge. Kendra smiles at me, but her dark shining eyes slip back to look at Royce. Jas and Cait share a plate of California rolls and a debate on whether journalism or broadcasting would be the better career choice. Do allergy sufferers make good broadcasters? The nasty little thought crosses my mind, and I would blush if my cheeks weren't already on fire.

"What do you think, Royce?" Jas flicks a grain of rice at him, "You goin' to college, or just be a hockey star? And you, Lex, any thoughts on what's next after school. Reporter, maybe?"

"Nnooo, not really," I stammer.

"Oh, think about it, Jas," Janey says, "She's going to be a photographer. For Planet and Nature." Janey beams her brilliant smile.

"I am?"

"Hey, you have lots of time to figure it out," Royce says, "So does Lame-Jane. You're still kids…uh, that is, you…" He sticks a sushi roll in his mouth then pushes the plate toward me. "Sushi?"

"Thanks," I say, looking up in time to see a black pick-up pull away from the curb across the street.

R. Rigsby

Day 4 Tuesday: Lewa
Out of the Frying Pan

Just when I convinced myself he was in Montreal, who knocks on my door as cool as winter in Tasmania, but Carlos? Impossible to pretend surprise.

"My bird," he says, "Give her to me now." He keeps one hand under his jacket, one of his old tricks. I keep one hand on the side of the door.

"I just have Lola." She fluffs her snowy feathers and raises her crest. "Mi querido!" she squawks. A familiar expression flashes on Carlos' face, but he lets it pass. Me too.

"You stole my bird, and you have her in that fine barn on your cousin's farm."

"She's not your bird, Carlos."

He shoots an arm out to grab me, but I dodge behind my door. He shoves a foot against it before I can push it closed. "No matter to me, and no matter to my friends. That payment will get my family out of that dung-hole village."

I lean on the door and gasp. "What 'friends' are you talking about? Fellow criminals? Besides, the bird is going to the South Carolina sanctuary. As soon as Tropic Watch makes the arrangements." A total lie. We have sent several parrots there, but I have no intention of sending the bird that far away.

A neighbour holding a watering can opens her door, and on the walkway, I catch a glimpse of, wouldn't you know it, Miss Alexis! Carlos sees her too and his jaw drops. Internal alarms clang. How would he know her? He looks from Alexis to my neighbour.

A stranger yelling outside a building in some places I've lived would attract no attention at all, but not in this town. Carlos, ever the charmer, salutes, and steps back.

"This isn't over." He keeps his voice low, and I can barely hear him above the noise of the truck upending the dumpster. "I'll get that bird. You can't keep it in that barn forever. We could do a deal. Especially if that young lady is who I think she is." I shut my door in his face.

The room in the loft is almost inaccessible now that the stairs are gone, so the bird is safe enough. He wouldn't dare threaten me through Alexis, but then he's not the man I once knew. When things come undone, they really come undone. Rightyo, new plan. Carlos' 'friends' could lean on him to be more forceful, or they could show up themselves. I need a new place to hole up. One where Carlos would never dream of looking. I have an idea, but it will involve some pleading. I make a call.

It goes better than I expected, and my guilt level rises accordingly. I call Mitch too, then cram my few things into my backpack. I invite Lola to step inside her carrier and load her into Mitzi, who sputters all the way to Maxine's farm. Mitch meets us at the back door of the stable.

"So what's up? Did you see that pick-up?"

"No. Carlos showed up at my door. And I should tell you he doesn't just want to talk to me–he wants the macaw."

"So that's it. That bird is valuable, isn't it?"

"Yes. And I'll tell Maxine that Carlos is out here."

We take Lola up to the room where she immediately opens a conversation with the macaw. As always, the sheer beauty of that bird quickens my pulse. She nickers answers to Lola's inquiries. I look out the windows but only see Cait trotting down the lane on Firefly.

At the house, I follow Mitch to the kitchen where Maxine pokes a fork into a pot in the oven. Roast beef. She scowls at me and raises her brows at Mitch.

No point delaying the news with inconsequential small talk. Has never been my strong suit anyway. "I left my apartment. Carlos found me, but I have a place to go."

Maxine's eyebrows almost meet her hairline and her mouth twists in that way I believe is reserved just for me. She slams the oven. "Carlos, *found you* Lewa? What exactly does that mean? If you work together, shouldn't he know where you are?" She clanks the long fork onto the counter.

"We parted ways, because of–"

"That bird? I should have known. I thought that letting you have the loft room was a way for us to be friends again. I should have known there would be complications. Lewa, I understand your, your, passion, but I never trusted Carlos."

"Once I get that bird to the conservatory, he'll leave me alone." *I hope it will be that simple.*

"Beth knows you're back. She called Saturday night. Alexis told her she met you. Beth didn't pursue it with Alexis and didn't mention it to Dawn. And now we have Carlos. What if Dawn sees him? I haven't even told her about you."

"They're not likely to meet in the grocery store, are they?" I can't help the exasperation. It's time for this whole thing with Dawn and Alexis to see the light of day. Dear God, the kid must have asked some questions by now. But I bite my tongue.

"Just a few more days. Everything is set up, and if I'm not here Mitch knows what to do. Cait can help."

"Cait can't help you. You know why." And right on cue, Cait comes in the door and sneezes.

"Sorry," she says. "What can't I help with?"

Mitch clears his throat. "Lewa has run into a few complications. Hey," he laughs, "she has been a walking complication from the get-go. It's just what she does."

My mouth falls open, but I realize Mitch is attempting a little levity and knows nothing of the circumstances of my birth. Maxine shakes her head, and Cait just stares at us. I get up to go, and at my head-jerk, Mitch follows me back to Mitzi.

"Thanks for helping there. I reckon your sister will do cartwheels when I finish up and go back east."

"Oh, that's just how she is. She's loyal to the family, but she hates how Dawn struggles to support herself and Alexis. And help Beth and Nick too. You should just call Dawn."

He's right, but I get into Mitzi without answering. This time, she stops as soon as I take my foot off the gas. Mitch takes over and coaxes her to run long enough to get up to the garage beside the house.

"Take my hatchback," he says, "and wear these, in case Carlos is watching." He hands me his cap and sunglasses. I wind my hair up underneath.

I leave Mitch reaching into Mitzi's engine compartment. My cousin is a good mate, but I haven't been honest with him. Maxine wants peace and Dawn might eventually forgive me. If I can get that bird to safety without messing up their lives again. But Maxine didn't invite me to dinner.

R. Rigsby

Day 7 Friday: Alexis
I Shouldn't Listen at Doors

I wake up freezing and shaking. A nightmare about facing a room full of grinning pumpkin faces. My throat was stuck. I couldn't speak a word and was blinded by the hair in my face. I heard snickering. I kept pushing my hair back and saying 'sorry,' which came out as a gagged chirp.

Flip's morning chitter under her blanketed cage brings me fully awake. I let her out, and she rides downstairs on my head. In the hall mirror, my heart flip-flops to see her, wings spread for balance and crest fully erect. She's one happy bird. Unlike me.

No school today, thanks to a teacher's professional day, but I don't have a topic. I spent all afternoon after school on Wednesday and Thursday in the school library. I looked at books on photography which made me feel like I know nothing despite taking thousands of pictures. I looked at books on cycling since I spend so much time on my bike, but that was even worse. Who knew there were so many kinds of bikes? And who cares? Mine is just a way of getting where I want to be. And even after poking about on the internet, I haven't found a subject I like.

I should do a talk on vacuuming. At least I feel something for it. Maybe I'll come down with mono. Or maybe I should rethink pet cockatiels. Still lame. Janey will speak about riding and caring for a horse, and the amount of time horses need. No surprise. She already has an outline and can hardly wait.

She's probably thinking about it right now while meeting up with Kendra and Rennie. They invited me to go shopping with them, but not much point with no money and tramping around the mall is boring. I think she has forgotten about Lewa, and I haven't brought it up. I didn't tell her about Cait's non-answer either.

Mum is at work and Flip helps me eat my Cheerios. She walks around the sheet of newspaper I put on the kitchen table, then hops on my arm. I scratch her head.

Cait asked if she could meet me at the library in town this afternoon. I said sure, why not, as if it didn't matter. Her class also has a year-end project and she's presenting something on running a farm, or stable, as a business. No kidding. She said she would meet me in the afternoon, after her allergist appointment. Something has really been setting her off lately. In more ways than one. I swear she backtracks and runs when she sees me coming. I call Mum as promised.

"Hi Honey, what are your plans today?"

"I'm going to work on my speaking project–I have an idea." Or rather, I wish I had an idea.

"Oh, that's great. I know you're worried." I hear the other line ringing." "Gotta go," she says. The usual zoo."

I pedal in top-gear to the stable but can't escape my conscience chirping at me, like Flip, for not being honest, again. I haven't told my mother about how I met Lewa in the loft. Cait asked me not to tell anybody, so six days of suppertime chat and not a word. But why is Lewa a big secret? Before I ask Mum about her best friend's mystery cousin, I want to know more about that cousin. Is there a reason nobody has never mentioned Lewa? And I want to find out what's in that room. I'm pretty sure I know, but I don't know why it's there.

The sun warms my shoulders and by the time I reach the driveway, the hair under my helmet sticks to my neck. Toady and Harley in the turn-out paddocks raise their heads.

"Not today." They'll give up on me if I keep whizzing by without an apple or a carrot. Lewa's van isn't at the back door. She mustn't be here. I lean my bike against the wall and hang my helmet on the bars. The door is open about a foot. Morning sun casts a long rectangle of light into the dusky interior. I peer in. The lights are on at the far end, where I see the wheelbarrow and fork, but no sign of Mitch. Or Brillo. And Cait sits in her allergist's waiting room. Lessons don't start until the afternoon, so no riders carry saddles, or groom horses.

It's a good thing I'm small. I slide through the door but freeze at the sound of voices. Somebody, or two somebodies, are in the tack-room. Mitch's voice for sure. Brillo must be near. The other voice is female. Maxine?

"…and I tell you Mitch, I'm sure the girl asked her mother or Beth–" Something clangs off a pail and I don't catch it all, but it's not Maxine, not with that accent. It's Lewa.

"About Carlos? What makes you think so?"

"No, not him or we would see Dawn circling the farm on her broom. I tell you Mitch, the girl knows something."

"Oh, come on, what makes you think so?"

"The purple headband. With sparkles."

"The what?"

"I found it outside the bird-room door Sunday evening. It was on her head on Saturday. She's been snooping upstairs. The door is locked now, but it wasn't then because Maxine was still looking for the key."

I touch my hair, thinking how silly that is. I thought my headband was buried in the manure pile. I should back out the door and pedal away, but I lean closer. Mitch is cleaning a saddle. I hear the soft whisper of a rubbing cloth and smell saddle soap. Brillo must be asleep. Or going deaf.

"I'm sure Cait hasn't told her. And so what if she knows? She's seen you and is likely to find out who you are eventually. Just because you found Alexis' headband doesn't mean she knows."

"No, Cait wouldn't tell. The sooner I get that parrot out of here, the better. Then I can leave."

"And you can't call the cops, right? Even about Carlos?" I pictured Mitch pushing his cap back and scratching his forehead.

"No papers, I don't own the bird."

"If the Mitz isn't fixed, I'll help you when you're ready to move it and…"

I don't listen to the rest of this sentence because I'm out the door. I know what's in that room, but why is it there? Is Lewa a parrot thief? A smuggler, like in the magazine? Are Cait and Mitch helping? Maxine must know. I'm sure I heard *Beth*. Would Auntie know? Who the heck is Carlos?

R. Rigsby

Day 7 Friday: Lewa
Flaming Unbelievable

Brillo, who was asleep on a saddle pad, lifts her head, curls her lip, and looks at the tack-room door. I shove it open and look outside in time to see–oh, who else would it be–Miss Alexis riding away on her bicycle, helmet bouncing from the handlebars.

"For Pete's sake. Can you believe this?" Mitch steps into the aisle beside me and together we watch her streak down the lane, her copper hair like strands of flame.

"I don't think it matters, Lewa. So, she knows you have a parrot upstairs."

"I didn't tell you. Carlos knows who Alexis is."

"What! How did that happen?"

"God knows. Maybe drove into her with his truck. Always was a wretched driver. When he came to my house, the little miss just happened to be wandering by. Incredible how she shows up. He recognized her. I don't want him to think he can get to me through her."

"Or rather, you don't want to involve Dawn? Or Beth and Nick?"

"Yes, well, about them–"

"You've talked to Beth and Nick?"

"I've done more than talk to them. I'm staying at their house."

"No kidding! I thought you were couch surfing with friends."

"What friends? Think about it, Mitch. I don't need all ten fingers to count the people I know out here. I called Nick when Carlos showed up."

"So, Beth and Nick are okay with everything?"

"No, not everything, especially in regard to Alexis, but we had a long talk. They're good people. They didn't deserve what I did."

"Lewa, why is Carlos so keen to get that bird?"

"Because he's taken money for her from some associates. I don't know who they are."

"So why not let Tropic Watch deal with him?"

"Because I'm not sure my contacts believe me, and even if they do, it'll take time. I'm not sure how much time I have to save that parrot."

"Well sure," Mitch says, "But have you thought about just giving Carlos the bird? Wouldn't a buyer who's willing to pay a lot of money afford to keep the bird properly? Give it a good home?"

"It's that kind of thinking that perpetuates the problem. People find that parrots aren't easy to keep healthy. Not everybody is prepared to give them the attention they need. And more birds suffer, they get sick, they die. And more birds are smuggled."

Brillo growls. Not liking my voice. Not liking the truth either.

Day 7 Friday: Alexis
About That Growing Nose

My bike clatters to the cement in the carport, front tire spinning, and I leave the back door open. For once I dropped the phone in its holder, so I don't run all over the house looking for it.

"Mum, I want to go to Auntie Beth's. I'm still working on my project." A big fat lie. "It's a nice day for a bike ride." I should see my nose ahead of me, growing like Pinocchio's.

"Oh, she and Uncle Nick will be delighted to see you. I'll call them to let them know you're coming. Watch the traffic."

It's farther to my aunt and uncle's than to the stable. I'm huffing and hot when I drop my bike and helmet against the back stairs. I find Auntie Beth in the kitchen, making sandwiches. She peeps at me over the top of her glasses.

"Well, well, look at you! Just in time for lunch. I have salad and ham sandwiches, and lemon loaf for dessert."

I make words come out of my watering mouth. "Did Mum call?"

"The whole world has called here today."

"Maybe I should have done that?" I stand beside Auntie at the sink where I wash my hands. I'm a tad taller than her! She's a small woman. Or maybe, I have grown. A late bloomer like Auntie says.

"Alexis, we are always happy to see you, call or no call. This is still your home. I didn't tell your uncle though." She turns and calls, "Nicholas, lunch is ready. And I have a surprise for you. Nichollaaas!"

Uncle Nick shuffles in from the living room. He has a magazine clamped under his arm and grins at me as he stuffs a hearing aid into each ear.

"I recognized the flying hair that zoomed past. I know you'll want to see this." He spreads the magazine, the latest *Planet and Nature*, open to the second part of the series on endangered parrots.

"Here's more evidence, as if we need it, about dwindling rain forests and the impact on eco systems. If the world doesn't smarten up, more birds will be gone, like the dodo. Just look at this—"

But Auntie places a platter of sandwiches on the table, so he shoves the magazine to the end of the table. I snorf lunch. It's been a long time since that bowl of Cheerios.

While Auntie plugs in the kettle and slices the loaf, I pick up the dishes, and stop to look again at the magazine. The germ of an idea takes root. Uncle Nick watches me, then with a crooked finger points to a picture of a blue and gold macaw flying through its jungly home, but the caption reads that not all parrots are so free, and their numbers are declining. The sidebar again mentions Tropic Watch and '*the dedicated members who struggle to prevent habitat loss and bird smuggling.*'

The lemon loaf and tea appear on the table and once again the magazine makes a polite retreat to the end of the table. Auntie asks me how school is going, as she always does, and if anything is new. She ignores her tea and slice of loaf and watches me take a big bite. Uncle Nick says something about mowing the lawn and excuses himself, taking his mug of tea and the magazine.

I open my mouth to ask Auntie about Lewa and what's going on in the stable, but she beats me to it.

"Something is on your mind, Alexis. Am I correct? Not that I'm not thrilled to see you but there's something you want to know. Something about a lady called Lewa if I'm not mistaken?"

R. Rigsby

Day 7 Friday: Alexis
Two Birds, One Lunch

My jaw drops open. "How did you guess?"

"I didn't need to guess. I remembered the conversation we had when you were here last week, and I have spoken to Lewa."

"You *know* Lewa?"

Auntie Beth lifts her teacup and sips. "I used to ride at the stable, a hundred years ago. Okay, not a hundred years, but it will seem like it to you. I've been friends with Cait's grandmother for years, and I know Lewa's parents. They often came out from Australia to visit. On one visit, surprise, Lewa arrived prematurely."

"Wow! Cait was premature too and almost didn't make it."

"Yes, well. Lewa's schedule rarely coincides with anybody else's. She's a survivor. And never fails to surprise." Auntie seems to say this to herself and takes a swallow of tea. "Your mother and Maxine have been friends since they were babies."

Auntie Beth and Uncle Nick raised Mum after my grandparents' accident. I must have looked like I was searching for a piece in a puzzle.

"Do you remember where your uncle worked before he retired?"

I nod. Fuzzy memories of the inside of a store, of shelves stacked with cans, boxes, plastic dishes, and bags of seed.

"In a pet shop." The smell of dog food in open bins, the sounds of chattering, barking, squawking came back too, and that smell–of birds. Parakeets, finches, and parrots–blue, red, green. I was only little at the time, but I loved them. Sometimes I dream about the shop.

"Yes, he did, for years. Before you were born, he had his own shop. He hired Lewa. She came out here to go to university."

"Was she allowed to work? Jas said his cousin came here on a visitor's visa and was busted for working. The government sent him home."

"She was born here–a citizen, so all legal. She joined the group that calls itself Tropic Watch while she was in Sydney."

My head snaps up at the mention of Tropic Watch–the sidebars in the series in *Planet and Nature*.

"You've read about them, I think?"

"Yes, but what does she do now? She has that room in the stable?"

"Ah, that. It was living quarters for the stable hands when the stable was built. There used to be an outside stairway which Maxine's parents knocked down. The room wasn't fit for people according to their insurance company. It's been empty for years."

"Cait told me about the room, but what about now? Where has Lewa been and why haven't I heard of her?" I wasn't letting this go.

"Lewa still works for Tropic Watch, but usually back east. She helps the organization find refuges for parrots of all kinds. Maxine has loaned her the loft room temporarily."

"And she has a bird in there now, right?"

"I believe so, just until wherever it's going has space. Then Lewa will leave too. That's all."

* * *

I pedal home slowly. For one thing, I'm tired, and for another, I have even more to think about. Or less. The whole Lewa thing is a simple deal, not a mystery. In the back of my mind, I see the black truck, but it can't be connected to anything. Nobody is hiding anything. Lewa is Maxine's cousin who rescues birds. And I have a topic for my speech.

The idea formed when I went to say goodbye to Uncle Nick. He wasn't mowing the lawn at all but was in his garden shed reading the magazine article. Perched around the shed are his collection of toy stuffed birds: ducks and owls, and a lot of parrots. Some have shiny plastic beaks and feet. One squawks like a pirate's parrot. He's had them for years. People used to give them to him.

Parrots. Of course. I would talk about them. And their habitat. And Uncle Nick could help–he knows about parrots and has read lots on bird protection and saving rain forests. He agreed that it would be fine topic. As a start, he said, I could have this magazine too.

My brain hums along in synch with my pedalling feet. Two problems, like two birds, my speech topic and Lewa the mystery lady, solved in the last hour. *Lewa!*

Oh, man, good idea! She knows about parrots. Time is running out. I need information fast. I need to talk to Lewa. Mum isn't home when I chain my bike in the carport. Should I call her at work? I hunt for the phone, but the back door opens.

"Mum!" She steps inside carrying an overflowing bag of groceries, her purse, and a jug of milk. "Do you know Lewa? The bird lady at the stable?" The jug of milk hits the floor. I dive for it as it bounces and rolls.

"It's okay, Mum, it didn't break!" I catch sight of Mum's face, which then goes quite still.

"Lewa? How do you know *her*?"

I notice the emphasis on '*her*,' but am too excited about my fantastic idea to think about it.

"I met Lewa last week. At the stable. Cait said not to say anything, but Auntie told me all about her."

"She did?" Mum hoists the grocery bag to the kitchen counter. She sits on a chair and looks at me. "Alexis. There's something I've been meaning to tell you for a long time. I should have told you years ago, but, you know, kept thinking you should be older."

"It's okay Mum. Auntie told me about Lewa. And about Uncle Nick's shop and about Lewa's birds."

"What birds?"

"You know, the ones in the room in the stable. She keeps them there while she finds them a refuge to go to. Auntie told me." Why doesn't she know about Lewa? But now that I have a topic, I need help. "I want to talk about parrots for my speech and I need to talk to Lewa. Auntie and Maxine know how to contact her."

Mum lets out a big breath. "Is that so? Let's fix dinner and talk about this later. Go get Flip so she can have some company."

I pause in the doorway and hear Mum mutter under her breath, "Still stealing birds, is she?"

After supper Mum first calls Auntie Beth and asks about Lewa. "I see," she says. I go on wiping dishes. "No, she hasn't called me. Yet. No, I understand why you couldn't. Yes, I'll call her next."

I put the dishes away and clean the sink. Mum calls Maxine. She sounds as if she's talking to a client about their bill. She hangs up the phone and smiles at me, but her dark eyes are granite.

"Maxine says if you can be at the stable tomorrow morning at eight, you may talk to Lewa."

Later, I sit at my desk. Parrots. What an amazing topic. Something I actually care about. I list some questions for Lewa and make notes from the magazine until Mum, on her way to bed, tells me to call it a night. I lie down, but my eyelids keep flipping open. When I finally start to doze off, I remember that I didn't ask Auntie about Carlos. I'll ask Lewa.

R. Rigsby

Day 7 Friday: Lewa
A Plan for Piper

After an afternoon with the birds, I go up to the garage to see how Mitch is doing with Mitzi. He says the van might be ready in a few minutes if I want to wait in the kitchen.

Maxine and I aren't exactly sharing a friendly cuppa, but we're civil. Does she remember boosting me onto her pony and treating me to lollies? So long ago when I was her favourite little cousin. The phone rings.

"I know, I'm sorry," Maxine says, "*It's Dawn*," she mouths to me.

I guessed as much. I wait for her to explain to her best friend why she hasn't revealed that her worst enemy, me, has crawled out of whatever abyss they imagined I lived in.

Instead, she says, "Yes, she's here right now." Maxine glares at me. "Can you meet with Alexis and talk about parrots? She's doing a school project."

Sure she is, crosses my mind, but I nod. I'll meet the kid. I'll give her the usual spiel for her speech or assignment or whatever it is, fifteen minutes, tops. No need to become best mates.

Maxine puts the phone down and her eyes glitter. I shrug. It's not my fault she thought she could keep this from Dawn. She goes out the door, passing Mitch. He wipes greasy hands on a rag.

"Sorry, no luck," he says.

"Dawn called." Mitch raises his brows. "Alexis knows about the bird. I'll see her in the morning."

"Good. Even with the insulation, a few clients have asked about the squawking from up there. I didn't think we could keep everything a secret for much longer."

I drive off, cap and sunglasses in place, thinking of the little Miss. For years, I thought she would be a little horror, spoiled by her mother and Beth and Nick, growing up as everybody's centre of attention, just because she's fatherless. Or maybe it was easier for me to think that. Lots of people survive without one parent or the other. Then that day in the loft. Those eyes. And she was so flustered and apologetic. Not the snotty brat I had envisioned at all, not that I haven't tried hard to hang on to that image.

I take a circuitous route to Beth and Nick's, as I have done since Tuesday, checking mirrors for a black truck, or any following vehicle. I drive straight into the backyard garage as Nick told me to do, beside their Ford Flex. He comes out of his shed, closes the overhead door, and I follow him across the grass to the kitchen. Beth pulls the blinds although it's barely twilight.

"I'll heat your supper," she says while sliding a large plate into the microwave. I carry on to the bathroom to wash and bring some semblance of order to my hair. Whatever is heating smells delicious. When

I sit down, she sets a teapot on the table. Nick lifts the lid and sniffs.

"Something herbal?"

"Camomile," Beth says. "Too late in the day for caffeine, and we are jumpy enough." She pours out three mugs. "Lewa, we must get this matter with Alexis and Dawn sorted. Alexis needs to hear the whole story, and Dawn needs to be the one to tell her. When you see Alexis tomorrow, please mind what you say."

I haven't told them I'll see Alexis in the morning. Beth and Nick have fingers on all the pulses. Between bites I say, "She only wants to know about parrots for a school speech. I have no intention of saying anything else. I wish I could have dropped that bird at the conservatory and then turned around and gone–"

"Where?" Nick asks, and my mind goes blank. "From what I gather, you might not have a job. And maybe it's time you thought about your future, with or without Tropic Watch."

"You're right. But no matter what I do, I need to deal with Carlos first."

Nick clears his throat. "Most people would call the police, but then they would want the 'evidence' and we need to get that evidence to a safe place first. There's a refuge an hour's drive from here."

"A good refuge? Not just a shed with ratty pens? I've seen lots of those. Run by people with good hearts, but not enough money to do it right."

"This one is right. They have secure funding and will be there for a long time. I volunteer there. Here's the manager's home number."

Nick watches my face when I call. The good news, they already have a macaw like Piper and would be delighted to have her. The bad news, they're short on quarantine spaces and can't take her for a week.

Nick nods when I tell him. "Yes, it's been a busy intake month. But Piper is safe in the stable room for now, right?"

"Right." I say, but not with confidence.

He and I talk more about bird rescue, and we have more in common than I believed. When he had the shop, he bought many birds, true, but then placed them in sanctuaries rather than selling them. He says he sold some birds, but only to knowledgeable buyers. He often talked to school groups or bird clubs, and still does.

Tucked up in the little bed that used to be Alexis', I recall how some pet-shop owners I knew were greedy no-conscience racketeers. They exploited a passion for exotic pets by people who had no idea how to care for them. Not just birds, but other creatures like monkeys, lizards, turtles, and fish that would outgrow any home aquarium. Most died. Nick was different. He has probably done more in years of education than I have in tracking down illegal importers in stinking warehouses. I just refused to see it.

I don't want any danger to come to Nick and Beth because of me, but I don't want to alarm them about Carlos' associates. Carlos might have told those associates I'm taking Piper to that South Carolina refuge. Maybe I should make that plan more convincing. It will buy me the week I need before moving Piper and it will keep me away from those I could endanger. That refuge just an hour or so away feels like it's on the moon, but it will be the best we can do for a parrot who should never have been taken from her forest home.

R. Rigsby

Day 8 Saturday: Alexis
Piper's World

I pedal like I'm in the Tour de France, and gravel shoots from my tires when I hit the lane. Once again, the back door of the stable is partly open, and once again I squeeze through. No van outside. Is Lewa here? Yes, at the foot of the stairs. She turns her head on one side.

Do I have a bug on my face? "What's wrong?" I say, then feel my face burning. "I mean, hello. Again."

"Hello again too. Nothing's wrong. You remind me so much of–somebody." Lewa's curly hair is red-brown, and she has it pulled back in a clip. Pale freckles spatter her nose and cheeks below grey eyes. I have grey eyes too, but my lashes are darker, and my hair has zero curl. Lewa wears the skirt and top from the other day, but no orange scarf.

"Oh, you live in town, don't you?" gushes out of my mouth before my brain catches up.

"You're quick, aren't you?" she says over her shoulder. I follow her up the stairs and ladder and along the catwalk. Lewa must be part cat.

She unlocks the door and waves me ahead. I gape at two parrots, each in a large cage. A cockatoo lifts its crest and blinks pearl black eyes. But the stunner is a brilliant hyacinth macaw. Sleek, blue feathers on the body and down the long, long tail. A circle of yellow around each bright brown eye and another patch of yellow near the beak. Gorgeous. I have seen pictures, and I saw one at a zoo, but not this close. The bird gazes at me and cocks its head as if wondering why the strange human has turned into stone.

The stone pulls out camera and notebook and looks around the room. The white walls are real walls, not boards like the rest of the stable. The door is thick and not a crack appears around it. The windows have louvered shutters, open to allow sunlight to fill the room. The tile floor shines damp from a recent mopping. A short counter holds a white sink. I look at the cages again.

"How did you get those cages up here?"

Lewa laughs. "I waved my magic wand. No, they were brought up here before the stairs were taken down and the doorway blocked in. They've been here for years."

How many years? flashes through my mind, but the macaw nickers. I giggle.

"Don't mind Piper. She was here only an hour and started with that. At least it's better than neighing. She can be loud."

"Piper. What a great name for–her? How can you tell?"

"It takes an expert. Or DNA testing. Which was done years ago."

I step closer to her and see what looks like a trail of dark gloop at the corner of the left eye. Not good, if she has runny eyes, but looking closer, I see it's a scar. I look at Lewa.

"An old injury."

"How long will these birds be here?"

"Piper is supposed to go to a public conservatory, but one of their birds has psittacosis, so I brought her here."

"Psittacosis isn't good. And contagious. I read about it in one of my parrot books." I look at the other bird.

"This is Lola. Let's get started, shall we?"

She tells me about the illegal trade of exotic species, especially parrots. Many die or are injured in the process. I make notes on how parrots are not easy to care for, and they live a long time. Not only do they need the right food and space, but because they are social and intelligent, they must have interaction and stimulation. With nothing to do all day, many develop bad habits, like picking out their own feathers.

I have read a lot about the usual pet birds like budgies and cockatiels. Flip has lots of toys, all made of bird-safe bits and pieces Mum and I make for her, but even now she's alone. Lewa sees my hand slowing down and stops talking.

"Sorry, thinking about my bird."

"What kind of bird?"

"Oh, just a cockatiel." I can't help looking at Piper and Lola.

"There's no such thing as *just* a bird. They are all special in their own way. Most are way smarter than dogs or cats. My first bird was a cockatiel too."

"Oh. I thought you…" but Lewa reads my mind.

"Alexis, Lola *is* my bird. I have papers for her. See her leg band; hatched right here in this country. She was a–a gift. I believe that large birds like Piper and Lola can be kept as pets, under the right conditions. But so many people who want a parrot don't understand their needs. They're a lot of work and there are no days off. For years and years. They aren't pets you can leave any place if you take a holiday. Some owners realize their pets are unhappy in too cramped spaces with not enough to do all day. It can be hard to cope. If they contact my agency, we try to find an alternative."

I look up from my frantic scribbling. I stick my pen in my teeth and stretch my fingers again.

"That's Tropic Watch, right?" I turn to a fresh page in my notebook.

"Yes, how did–never mind." Lewa stands up and goes to one of the windows.

"Does Tropic Watch pay for the birds?"

Lewa turns to face me and leans against the window ledge. She puts both hands in the pockets of her skirt. "Not usually. But some are worth thousands."

"I read that hyacinth macaws are among the most expensive of all parrots." I can't help looking at Piper again. "Is this all you do?" I pick up my camera and click off a few shots. "Take unwanted birds to sanctuaries? What about smugglers?" *Click check, click check.* I'm getting some great pictures. "Do you stop people who smuggle parrots?"

Lewa blinks but smiles as she pushes back a few strands of hair that escaped the clip. I know that feeling.

"Tropic Watch is a large organization involved in many aspects of saving the world's parrots and habitat. They work with police and border patrols to stop smuggling, in accordance with CITES, the Convention on International Trade of Endangered Species."

"Oh." She sounds like she's reading from the magazine. "Was Piper rescued? My aunt says you work in Ontario. Wasn't there a place for her there?" Lewa breathes in deeply. I think she's about to tell me to mind my business.

"Alexis, part of my job with Tropic Watch is to rescue birds in danger. Piper was in danger, and I took her from the person who had her."

My eyeballs feel like they might pop out. "Tropic Watch told you to do that?"

"No. The situation was urgent. He was about to turn her over to a smuggling ring for a lot of money. I had to act. There wasn't time for Tropic Watch to intervene." She closes her eyes for a second and shakes her head. "When I left Kingston, I called Tropic Watch, but only said I found Piper and was taking her to safety. I didn't explain how I came to possess a missing and very valuable bird."

"And you came all the way in that van? With Lola too?"

"We made it in three nights and the Mitz chugged right along. At least until the last stretch. I only stopped for gas, food, and a few hours sleep."

"Who had Piper? And why?"

"She should have been in a refuge, and I couldn't believe it when I learned she was about to be sold, and maybe not for the first time."

Again, Lewa doesn't answer my question. At least not that question, but now hiding a parrot in a loft makes sense.

"Listen, Alexis, I shouldn't have told you that and it's best you keep it to yourself."

I look at my camera in my lap. "I was here yesterday morning."

"I know."

"I thought you were a bird smuggler."

"It's been my life's work to stop smuggling."

"Like Piper?"

I would love to tell you Piper's whole story. Just not today, yes?"

Piper hops to the side of her cage and sticks her beak through the bars.

"You can give her a treat." Lewa reaches behind her and pops the lid on a plastic container. Banana chips! "Here, give her one of these, but be careful. She's friendly, but you need to be cautious."

Not to be outdone, Lola bobs her head. "Hello, mate," she says.

I laugh. "Does she say anything else?"

Lewa holds out banana chips for her. "Yes, heaps, but that's her favourite."

I watch Lewa, then hold out the chip to Piper. She plucks it from my fingers. As she munches, I poke my finger through the bars and massage the spot where her ears would be if she had them, just like I do on Flip. I hear Lewa's sharp intake of breath, but Piper gurgles something in happy parrot speak and leans into my fingers, closing her eyes.

"Blimey. That's wonderful. You have the magic touch."

I rub Piper's head, and her neck as far as my fingers will reach, then offer her another banana chip.

She leans in for another scratch. Such a great bird. I would love to take her home.

"When do you think she will go?"

"I don't know for sure." Lewa pauses, then says, "There's a refuge in South Carolina. The climate would be good for her and I'm leaving tomorrow to visit it."

"Were you saving birds when you worked for my Uncle Nick? Was Carlos there too?" I just remembered I wanted to ask about him.

I look up in time to see Lewa reshape her face.

"Yes, rightyo, he's a good man, your uncle." Her phone buzzes and she looks at the screen. "We have a few more minutes." While I resume scribbling, Lewa explains more about how parrots are captured and taken from the rain forests, and as if this weren't bad enough, bad mining and forestry practices destroy their habitat. She doesn't answer my question about this Carlos guy.

"How long have you been doing this?" If she worked for Uncle Nick years ago when she was a student, she could be about thirty-five, like my mother. Maybe younger.

Lewa shrugs. "Too long." She was looking at her phone again but looks up at me. "The job isn't as glamourous as you might think. Sometimes it's sad, especially when birds die, and you find out not everybody cares as much as you thought they did."

"Uncle Nick had parrots in the shop where he worked. Now he only has stuffed birds. Did you work with him when he retired?" What I'm really asking is where has she been all this time.

"Well, ah, no. I left before then." Her phone buzzes again. "I'm sorry Alexis, I need to take this call." She asks the caller to hold a minute.

I put my notebook and camera in my backpack. One day, I might hear the whole story, whatever it is, but now I can write up the report. I'll worry about delivering it without fainting later. Lewa. So calm, with her mass of curly hair, and cool clothes. She has what must be the best job in the world. Piper and Lola adore her.

"Alexis, it would be best not to mention my name in your speech." I nod and leave. At the foot of the ladder, I almost land on Cait.

"So, you met Piper," she says. "I hate keeping secrets. Especially from friends."

"Ohhh...I'm sorry, the library, I forgot."

"De nada," she waves her hand, looking nonchalant, then sneezes, ruining the effect.

"Oh, Cait, maybe you should take a pill?"

"Nah. I'm fine. And if you think hay makes me sneeze, you should see me in action around Lewa's birds."

Day 8 Saturday: Alexis
Fitting the Pieces

We part at the foot of the stairs and Cait goes back to her wheelbarrow. Janey will be here soon. In fact, she's late. I fetch Pinball's tack, and then bring him in from the paddock. I put a handful of oats in his bucket and start grooming.

The rhythm of brushing, brushing, down Pinny's neck, across his withers, his back, and down his legs should settle the thoughts jumping around my brain. Over and over. Pinball sighs and munches. I should be relaxed too. Cait and I are friends. I solved the mystery of the bird room. Lewa is amazing. I have everything I need for my talk. I again think of Flip.

This morning, while she helped me eat breakfast, I asked her if she would rather be free with other cockatiels. Cockatiels live in wild flocks in Australia. Is Flip happy with just me and Mum for company? When she *has* company? I'm at school, Mum works, so most of her day she waits alone in her cage. Is that fair? She fluffed her feathers, stretched, and opened her beak as if to make a grand pronouncement. Instead, she yawned. I scratched her head and said, "Okay, that's settled, then."

But now I wonder, while stroking Pinball's face, is Flip happy? Pinball goes out to the fields every day and visits his horse friends. He's ridden often and gets lots of pats and treats. Is he happy?

I have much to be happy about. Flip and Pinball, Mum, Auntie and Uncle Nick, and my friends. And now Lewa. The hippest friend ever. How lucky I am, really. So maybe this Father's Day won't bug me. I had a father, for long enough to make me, but Mum said he was gone before I was born. He's probably dead, like my grandparents. Janey's known from kindergarten that no male parent is in the picture, and she has never asked me about it. Neither has Cait, and Bill is away so much, he may as well not be here. Not a big deal. We all know kids with only one parent.

So much has worked out, but I'm missing something. Like when I lost a tooth–my tongue thought it should be there, but it wasn't. If my father is dead, shouldn't my mother have told me? Or Auntie Beth and Uncle Nick? They often tell stories about my grandparents. Why doesn't anybody talk about my father?

I thought I had the Lewa mystery figured out. Brushing Pinny has given my brain time to come up with more questions. She didn't say anything about Uncle Nick. Why not? She wasn't here when he retired. Where did she go?

I brush slower and slower and stop altogether at the sound of a vehicle pulling up and voices. Janey and Royce play-shove each other as they squeeze through the stall door.

"Hey thanks, he looks great! Whoa, I need to move, or we'll be late." Janey swings the saddle and blanket onto Pinball.

"Oh, I think that earns a double ride today," says Royce. "How are you doing, Alexis? Is the newsletter ready to go?"

"It is, I'm great, and I'll take whatever ride I can get." Words and laughter flow out of my mouth without stuttering, and I don't automatically push my hair off my face. It is in my face, but instead of looking at my boots, I look up at Royce and smile. Kendra, Shmendra.

"Gotta go," Royce says, at the sound of the horn. "Dad's taking me to the rink–last practice and next week the last game before they take out the ice. See ya, Lex. You too, Sis."

* * *

We're in Pinball's stall after Janey's lesson and another hour of taking turns hacking around the back field. I sit on my favourite overturned bucket while Janey grooms. Cait clumps around in the loft, and the snorts of hungry horses greet flakes sliding down chutes.

"So, tell me what's bugging you," Janey says.

I had to tell her about meeting Lewa. There was no way to explain how I had come up with the topic for my speech, and how I had so much great information so fast. Lewa didn't exactly say not to tell anybody, she'd prefer I didn't mention her in my talk. Maybe it's my face, but Janey knows when I'm thinking.

"I don't know. I'm so relieved about my speech and will start writing it out tonight. Maybe this afternoon. After vacuuming. I'm glad the creepy ladder and catwalk in the loft don't lead to a torture chamber. It's just an old room now used to keep a few birds. Lola is sweet, but I wish you could see Piper."

"I'll stick to horses, thanks. I like Flip, but big birds make me nervous." Janey stops swiping Pinball's already gleaming sides and puts a hand on his hip. "So, Lewa is a bird-lady, the loft room is a bird-house, your uncle is an ex-bird-man, but you feel like a bird-brain because you're not happy with the explanations? What else?"

"Mum dropped the milk. At the time I was so anxious to meet Lewa, I didn't pay attention. Mum never drops a thing."

"Whoa, a sure sign something is off. You should hire a private investigator."

"No, really, it was the look on her face when I mentioned Lewa. She was shocked, and for a moment, she looked scared."

"Your mother? Scared?" Janey drops the brush in the caddy and looks at me. "Then you should just ask her." Janey, despite her laughing ditzy way, can be hard-headed and practical.

I leave her to finish up on her own, and ride homeward. My bike might be just a means to get back and forth, but pedalling prompts thinking, which is good if I keep an eye out for parked trucks. Why didn't Auntie Beth tell me more about Lewa? There seems to be a huge gap between her working for Uncle Nick and now, like my whole life. She never once visited her cousins Mitch and Maxine, and Bill and Cait?

And that conversation I overheard between Mum and Maxine last week. I thought they were talking about Auntie Beth, but why just 'her' and not 'them'? Wouldn't Uncle Nick be included? Or maybe it wasn't about them at all. Then Mum said something about having to tell me something she should have told me a long time ago. About what? Was I adopted? Found in a basket at the bottom of Uncle Nick's garden? Does this Carlos guy have something to do with me? Like being the missing paternal unit? Janey said I should just ask. Tonight, when Mum comes home from work.

R. Rigsby

Day 8 Saturday: Alexis
One Surprise After Another

I'm surprised to see our grey Toyota in the carport when I get home. Mum should be at work for at least another hour. I chain my bike and open the door as if it were wired for a bomb. Maybe she has one of her migraines.

"How could you not tell me Lewa is here?"

Mum has no headache, but she's explosive, and she has company. I shrink behind the door. Something else I'm getting good at.

"Now Dawn, she's my cousin." Maxine. "I loaned her the old room because she was stuck. She had an apartment in town, but she had to leave it."

"Well so it seems, as you say she is living at my aunt's house. I can't believe Auntie hasn't told me."

"Lewa had a long talk with Beth and Nick. They took her in when Lewa had some, ah, difficulty with an old acquaintance.

"Carlos?" Maxine must have nodded, and Mum goes on. "Carlos is out here too? Oh, the man has nerve. Lucky me, Carlos *and* Lewa."

"I just learned about Carlos, but when Lewa arrived, I didn't tell you because I knew you would worry that Alexis might meet her. And she did. I'm sorry about that. I started to tell you last week. We were interrupted, but really, you should tell Alexis her father exists."

My knees buckle and I lean against the wall. My father is alive? Carlos? The guy who left a long time ago? Maxine knows him. Who else? Well just about everybody I bet. I can't help the quick breath.

"Alexis! How long have you been there?"

"Long enough to hear my father isn't dead and long enough to figure out that everybody but me knows who he is." I'm shouting. It feels great. "He wasn't a guy you met at a party and I'm just the result of a bad decision, like I've thought for years. And years."

I don't sense my hand reaching for the doorknob but there it is in my fingers, certain, solid. Maxine steps toward me, and I yell at her."

"Cait knows all about this, doesn't she? Like she knew about Lewa and didn't tell me. I'm the biggest idiot ever." I wondered if the comments about my looks, hair, eyes, were people comparing me to the man they knew.

"Alexis, wait," Mum reaches out.

I stop with my back against the door. My hand still clutches the doorknob. "Why didn't you tell me about him right from the beginning? If he knows Lewa, he knows everybody, and everybody knows him."

My mother who is always the calmest, most composed person in my life looks like she's coming apart. All that secrecy kept inside for years, now about to spill. And not just her keeping the secret–Maxine, Mitch, Auntie, Uncle Nick, and Cait too. Why? Where does Lewa fit in?

"Alexis, I thought it hopeless. I believed he could never be part of your life. Why tell you about a father you would never meet? I never lied to you, but I haven't told you the whole story. I'm sorry it had to happen like this. I was wrong to keep it from you."

But I'm already out the door. I slam it behind me and pedal halfway down the block before I hear Mum call me to come back. I'm not the pathetic orphan after all; I'm even more pathetic, I have a father who hasn't looked for me my whole life. I don't want to know him either, but there's one person I can talk to now.

R. Rigsby

Day 8 Saturday: Lewa
Now That Has Me Thinking

I'm watching out the windows again, which I do every ten minutes, it seems like, when I'm with the birds. I see no black truck or any other vehicle remotely suspicious.

Alexis has been gone for an hour and I'm sorry she left. This morning, I wasn't really watching for her, but I saw her way up the road, pedalling like she was in a race.

I didn't expect her to be so earnest. Or have a pet cockatiel like I had. Piper, who is usually reserved with strangers, loves her. I didn't expect so many questions either. Alexis quickly grasped the environmental issues, and I'm surprised by how much I enjoyed talking to her. But her questions have me questioning myself. I'm not getting any younger, and, like Nick says, I need to think about what's next once I deal with Carlos. No more falling for his smooth charm. I lied to Alexis about South Carolina, but in case Carlos corners her, it's a good place for her to believe me to be.

Alexis wants to hear more of Piper's history, but that would include my own sorry past. Yesterday, I didn't care what she thought, but this morning, it hit me that she isn't just a curious kid I will never see again. I was tempted to tell her the *real Lewa* story. The repeated calls from Tropic Watch saved me from confession.

I wrapped up the interview with Alexis even though I wanted her to stay. I hope when she learns what I did, she'll give me another chance. Tropic Watch gave me another chance, and now I've pushed my luck with them again.

"Lewa!" echoes in the rafters.

I open the door to see Mitch's head above the anteroom. "Can you come to the garage?"

When I get there, he shuts the engine compartment and says good news, the stalling problem is fixed, but bad news, one of the rear tires is flatter than the outback. He doesn't use those words, but that's how it looks.

"Where's your spare?"

"I traded it for gas to a farmer in Saskatchewan. Nice old bloke. Richard something. I was short on cash."

Mitch pushes his cap back–a different cap since I'm still using his other one–and runs a hand through wispy hair.

"Okay, I can get one for you. What are you using for money these days? Not that it's my business."

"Right, not your business, but, yeah, funds are tight. I'm okay for now."

"You can pay me for the tire whenever, and if you need a loan in the meantime, say so."

"Will that tire be on later today? I need the Mitz for sure tomorrow."

"Why? I haven't known you long, but I have a feeling you're up to something."

"When I told Tropic Watch I had Piper, they demanded explanations, or they would involve the police. I said I was driving and would check in at the first opportunity. They weren't expecting that to take a week, but I left a message for my contact this morning, who kept buzzing me just before Alexis left."

"And they know about Carlos now? But you're still up to something?"

I tell him my plan to lure Carlos on a wild goose chase. Or a parrot chase. "I want him to see my van leaving and follow me to the airport."

"Sounds bonkers, but okay. I better find you a tire. Come on Brillo."

"And I better get upstairs and finish with the birds."

I open their cages. Lola climbs to the top and preens as if it's something she can't possibly do inside. Piper looks out her door. She pauses for a minute, as if considering, but then she too climbs up and flaps her wings. Lola gets into the act, and they have a good flap together. They have me laughing as they always do, and these days a good laugh is rare.

I'm still laughing when I look out the window and see Alexis, again pedalling up the lane, helmet bouncing and hair flying. She might be coming back to see her friend, who has left, but no, I hear her pounding up the stairs.

R. Rigsby

Day 8 Saturday: Alexis
Getting the Story Straight

I don't think about the height when I reach the catwalk. Lewa opens the door. When I reach her, she shuts it behind me, and I fall into her arms. I think I'm panting, but I'm sobbing. She hugs me and pats my head, then steers me to a chair.

"Here, sit." A tissue appears in my hand, and I snort into it. Water runs and Lewa presses a glass into my fingers. She brings the other chair over and sits in front of me. Both birds look at me with anxious bird faces. I smile at them through bleary eyes. Lewa looks over her shoulder at the birds and smiles too.

"Right. Tell me what happened."

I have a feeling she already knows, but as I blubber the story her expression varies from understanding to surprise.

"…And the worst part is that everybody but me has always known about my father." I hiccup. I've stopped sobbing, but my eyes are in flood. I honk a few more times into the soggy tissue. Lewa hands me another. She picks up her bag from the counter, takes out her phone and jabs at it.

I haven't cried like this since I was ten and fell out of the pear tree in Auntie's yard. At least my sprained wrist hurt, and I had something to bawl about.

Why am I bawling now about some guy I'll never meet? "You know Carlos, don't you?"

"I do. Alexis, you really shouldn't jump to conclusions when you listen at doors."

"He's my father, isn't he? Why hasn't anybody told me about him? I thought Mum maybe didn't know who my father was."

"Your mother? No way. She was never like that. And I can assure you Carlos is *not* your father."

A hot wire jabs my brain. *He's not?* Then who is? I jump up knocking over the chair. Lola screeches and both birds lift their wings. "But you know, don't you?"

"Sit down Alexis, you're upsetting the birds."

I don't sit down, but I pick up the chair and send mental apologies to Lola and Piper. That was childish. The birds don't deserve a fright like that.

"Alexis, you need to hear the whole story, which I think your mother was getting to. I agree you should have known long before this, but…" Her phone buzzes. "Your mother is coming. We'll meet downstairs." She stands up and holds her arm out to Piper who steps onto it and then into her cage. Lola flaps and climbs down.

"See ya," she says.

I smile at her even though anger seethes through my innards. "I'm not going anywhere until you tell me about my father."

Lewa bolts the cages, then turns to me, hands on her hips. "Alright."

Really, flashes through my mind. *She's going to tell me?*

"Your mother will strangle me, but here goes."

I expect a theatrical sigh, and a melodramatic flourish, and maybe the name of a college fling who couldn't deal with parenthood. Instead, Lewa shrugs and speaks quietly.

"Your father is my brother. Alexander. You have his eyes and are obviously named for him."

"But, but…"

"Let's go down." Lewa looks like Lola when she had to go back in her cage.

Maxine in her truck tears past us and shakes her head at Lewa. We're standing at the back door near the foot of the stairs. In Maxine's dust, my mother's car comes up the lane and stops in front of us. Mitch will give her heck for parking there. I wonder where Cait is. She might be finished for the day. I have the wild idea of running up to the house to see her and let Mum and Lewa do their thing.

Mum, still wearing her work scrubs, gets out. "You told her, didn't you, Lewa?"

I always suspected my mother could read minds. At least my mind.

"I made her tell me." The first words I've spat out since learning that Lewa has a brother, who was, is, my father.

"Alexis, you need to hear everything."

"Come inside," Lewa says, leading the way to the tack-room.

Lewa and Mum glare at each other from either end of the room. I sit on my overturned bucket and wait.

"I'll start from the beginning," Mum says, "Even though what happened then wasn't Lewa's fault. Before

Lewa was born, Lewa's mother came here to visit. Everybody was at the farm for dinner when Lewa's mother went into labour. My parents drove her to the hospital. On their way back to get me, a semi coming down the highway blew a tire and slammed into them."

Mum and Auntie told me about the accident when I first asked them why I had no grandparents. I grew up knowing my mother was orphaned before she was three and Auntie Beth and Uncle Nick raised her. Does Mum hate Lewa because her sudden birth caused my grandparents' deaths? What has that got to do with stealing birds, like my mother said?

Mum leans against a saddle stand and looks at me. "Auntie Beth and Maxine's mother are good friends. Maxine and I grew up together. Kind of like you and Cait. Maxine and I started university together, then went to Sydney to do a semester there. We stayed with Maxine's aunt and uncle and her cousins, Alex and Lewa."

Lewa stares at the floor. "When Maxine and I came home, Alex came too and took a job at the Aquarium. He was finishing his degree at the university, and I was studying to be a vet. Then Lewa came–"

"I'll take it from here," Lewa says. "Alexis, I have loved birds all my life, even before my first cockatiel. When I joined Tropic Watch, I learned the truth about exotic pet birds, and I couldn't do enough to help. Some of us were very, um, enthusiastic and I was included in missions to stop smuggling, not always with Tropic Watch's blessing. When I ran out of money, your Uncle Nick offered me a job at his store. I argued with him a lot about the ethics of keeping parrots. I know now he ran a good shop, and his birds weren't smuggled or traded, but at the time it was hard. I felt that every parrot should be restored to a forest home. So naïve."

I could picture Lewa arguing.

"Poor Uncle Nick was only trying to make a living," my mother says. "He checked all his buyers, but you were young and hot-headed."

Lewa looks out the door. I look too, but only see Firefly with her head over the stall gate. Does Lewa see wild parrots flying through treetops? Then Lewa says, "I took your uncle's keys. I stole his car and broke into his shop."

"You wanted to steal the parrots and take them to refuges. I guess we know who suggested that," Mum says.

"There was a little more to it, but the result was the same. I would have got away except Nick's car stalled and wouldn't start. I called Alex." She looks at my mother.

"You shouldn't have come with him."

"Why wouldn't I? And none of us knew that a man walking his dog in the alley saw you in the back of the shop and got suspicious. He called the police. You should have listened to Alex."

"I wasn't very good at listening then. All I wanted to do was to get that bird to safety. I thought Tropic Watch was willing to help. When your mother and Alex went inside to call Nick, I heard the sirens, so I put the bird in Alex's car and took off."

"Here?" I say.

"Carlos said he would meet me here. I thought we were doing a wonderful rescue of a bird in peril. Carlos didn't show, but the police did."

"Uncle Nick would have dropped the charges," Mum says, "but the stolen parrot wasn't his–it was just boarding–and its owner was enraged. It was a rare and valuable bird. And the insurance company wouldn't pay if Uncle Nick didn't press charges."

I hear all the words, including the bit about 'a rare and valuable bird,'–*Piper*? But there's another level of meaning I'm missing. I've heard a lot about Lewa, but really, all ancient history. I'm still waiting to hear about my father. I do the math and figure I must have been conceived about that time.

"I don't care about any of that! Where is my father, Alexander, now?" Hot red words erupt in my head, flow out of my mouth. "Did he leave when he found out about me? And if not, where is he? If he's not dead, why hasn't he tried to see me?"

Lewa straightens her shoulders, stands up and goes to the door. "I'm going up to the birds." She turns and looks at me. "Because he tried to help me when I committed a crime, Alex got sent back to Australia."

Day 8 Saturday: Alexis
More Revelations

I look at my mother. "Before you ask, Alexis, we did try to stay together. But I was implicated in Lewa's crime and Australia refused my visa."

"And you had me?" I say to Mum.

"Yes, at least you were on the way. So, there we were–Alex and I separated by an ocean, and an ocean's worth of angry words. I was flaming furious with Lewa. Furious with Alex for trying to help her and dragging me with him."

I try to imagine my mother in a hot fury. I've never seen it although I've given her lots of reasons. When I was twelve, I snitched money from the grocery tin for a cherry lip gloss like Rennie's. A December day in the arctic spread through the house when Mum missed the money, and I had a whole weekend in my room to think about why taking money we needed for food was a bad idea.

"I was furious about what happened to Uncle Nick," she says, and reaches down to take my hands. "My dear Uncle, who tried to help Lewa, repaid like that. The bird's owner slammed him with a lawsuit for 'stress' to her bird she said. Uncle Nick lost the shop and had to take a job in another store. By then I had told Alex to get on that plane and not come back; that it was best if we each got on with our lives alone. I didn't want help; I didn't want to hear from him. I couldn't see any solution."

"And you never tried again?"

"Yes. Often. So did he. When we came to our senses, we knew we owed it to you to keep trying, but it was hopeless. Neither of us could travel. We thought it would be hard on you, so we have gone for years without talking, and really, I think…" My mother sighs and looks away. "When Alex tried to contact me, I refused to talk to him. It wasn't fair or right, but I was punishing him instead of Lewa. I had to quit my vet studies because there was no money after Uncle Nick's lawsuit. But, Alexis, this is what I've been wanting to tell you. Alex is again trying to get a visa. He called Uncle Nick and asked him to speak to me. He wants to come here and meet you. I talked to him last Saturday."

The call I interrupted. No wonder she didn't give me a hard time about the vacuuming.

"Why try to come back now after all this time?" This time the eruptions have flames. The nerve. "He takes off on us and then thinks he can just fly back into our lives. And you're okay letting him do that?" I'm ready to bolt for my bike again and go find, well, not Lewa, but somebody sane and normal. Janey would do. Royce would be better. I pull my hands free. "Everybody but me has known all along–*you* should have told me!"

I hear muffled squawks from Lola and Piper upstairs. Nobody explains anything to them either. Like other captive parrots, they have no choice in what happens to them, and I want people to know that. I'll add that to my speech while it's fresh in my head, even though this morning's interview feels like years ago. I stand up. I'm hot and sweaty and my hair hangs in my face. I hate that too. I'm getting a haircut.

"Mum, I'm going home. I'll ride my bike." At home, I shower and go straight to my room to write my speech. Mum doesn't drag me out for dinner.

R. Rigsby

Day 9 Sunday: Alexis
No Rewind on Life

Janey isn't at the stable when I go to work. She was drafted to go and watch Royce's last game. Most of the horses are out in the paddocks or being ridden, and the stable feels empty and strange. Much like my innards. Mitch's scrawl on the white board says no turn-out for Ace as he has gone lame and needs stall rest. He and Cait have gone to look at a possible lesson pony. I want to talk to Cait. She must know about my father. *Alexander*.

He wants to meet me. I guess Lewa will leave soon, and our lives could go back to how they were before. If I refuse to meet him.

Minou strolls down the aisle and mews greetings. I pick her up. Soothing purrs resonate against my ribs. I carry her to the feed-room and put her on the oat bin before picking up the fork and shovel.

I stab filthy straw and manure and bang my pitchfork on the edge of the wheelbarrow with every deposit. Lewa could have told me about her past–a past with me in it. Even if I was microscopic. Anger fills that hollow space in my innards. Mucking out stalls is almost as good for thinking as biking, and as I fork and rake, I think about my new relatives in two countries.

Lewa for one. My aunt. She hurt my mother, Auntie and Uncle Nick, and my father. I wonder if he's still angry with Lewa. My life would have been a lot different if it weren't for *My Aunt*. When we met yesterday, she didn't say a word about how she ruined five lives. Not even *Hey Alexis, there's something you should know about me. I might not be the megastar you think I am.*

I upend each wheelbarrow load and bang it down onto the ramp with as much strength as I can. I'm a little girl patted and protected by people who should have told me about my father. Ace pins his ears when I clank by after the fifth load.

"Sorry, buddy." I stop, then go to the feed-room for a handful of oats. I stroke his neck while he munches. "Noisy, aren't I? Never mind, I'm better now." Even if I knew every syllable of the *Life of Lewa Story*, including that Carlos guy, would it make any difference? I think of the clocks I doodle. Time never ticks backwards.

I'm in Firefly's stall when I hear Piper's raucous calling above the distinctive putt-putt of Lewa's funny little van pulling up at the back door. We can't miss seeing each other. I look up and swipe hair out my eyes and she does too. Her hair is clipped back, but stray curls sit on her cheeks, and in the soft light she looks younger. Or maybe it's her expression, like a little kid who's been bad. I crook a half-smile and lean on my shovel.

"You have more questions, don't you?" she says.

"I think I figured it out. Piper was the bird you stole from Uncle Nick, and you must have gone to jail, or did they boot you out of the country too?"

"Jail. I'm a citizen so they couldn't boot me out. And yes, I stole Piper."

"Why?"

Lewa sighs. "If I didn't do something, my sweet girl would go back to a lonesome cage. I stole Piper then, and I stole her again last week.

"From Carlos. He's a smuggler, isn't he?"

"Yes. And he's in deep trouble with some rough characters. He's desperate to get Piper back because they have paid him a lot of money for her. That's why I'm doing whatever I can to get her to a sanctuary. I'm leaving now for that refuge in South Carolina. I'll be gone until Saturday. We can talk more about this later, yes?"

"Sure. But Lewa. Even if Piper is saved, it won't stop Carlos from stealing other birds. Or smuggling. Or his friends from doing that." I feel my cheeks warming. I'm not the expert here. Lewa looks at me, then looks out the door.

"Mitch will see to the birds; I'm just dropping their food before I go." She holds up a bag before turning and going up the stairs. Her footsteps echo, and then they stop.

"Alexis, you're right," she calls down, and the footsteps, quicker now, recede.

I fork more dirty straw into the wheelbarrow. A few minutes later, I'm in the feed room putting away tools. I hear Lewa opening her van and I stick my head

R. Rigsby

out in time to see her slam the door on a large carrier. I don't wave when she leaves.

Day 9 Sunday: Lewa
Decoy Tactic

Everybody believes I'm on my way to South Carolina to inspect a new refuge, and if Carlos questions anybody, that's the story he will hear. Of course, with my record there's no way I can cross the border. Carlos knows that, but we used forged passports before. If I'm lucky, he'll believe I have Piper, with fake papers, and he might go to South Carolina himself.

I drive Mitzi into the airport parking lot. For a few minutes I watch the rear-view mirror. A blue sedan, a grey van, a silver SUV, and a green two-door with the back windows blacked out. Drivers get out, take bags, and walk away. No black ute. Carlos or one of his mates could have a different vehicle, but if they watched from one of those that arrived after me, they would be half-cooked. June is lovely in this hemisphere.

I wind up my window and get out. A few minutes later, I walk into the terminal wearing my backpack and carrying a covered carrier. I pass the check-in counters, go down the escalator, out the arrivals door, and onto a bus for the city. The driver lifts his eyebrows at the carrier, but I show him it contains a pair of boots.

I take a room at a fleabag hotel where I will spend the next six nights. Piper is as safe as she can be in the bird room with all doors locked and Mitch bedding down in the tack-room with Brillo, even if she is going deaf. I hope my disappearing act, if it doesn't draw Carlos away, will at least make him wonder what I'm up to. I would like to know what *he* is up to. Why so keen on getting Piper? Surely, with his network, there are lots of other birds to steal.

Day 9 Sunday: Alexis
Who's Calling?

I bike home, but Mum is out. I start upstairs for a shower when the phone rings. I don't look at the display.

"Hello."

"Is this Miss Alexis Jensen?" A man. My father? My insides do a back-flip.

"Yes, yes, it's m,m,me," I stammer and can't believe the heat rushing to my face. "Is this A,a,Alex? D,d,dad?" There is dead air on the other end of the phone. Did I lose the connection?

"Ah, no, I am calling from Tropic Watch. I'm trying to contact Lewa Hosford. Would you know where she might be?"

"South Carolina," I babble before thinking. She couldn't be there yet. The surprise of possibly speaking to my father subsides and allows the thinking part of my brain to rise to the top. Who is this? The voice sounds familiar. Here's where I should ask a whole lot of questions about who's calling. I hear throat clearing on the other end of the call.

"Oh, I see. Do you happen to know when she left?"

Lewa said Tropic Watch asked her to go there so why call to find out? And why here? My neck hairs prickle.

"Her plane left earlier today." In a flash of understanding, I add, "She took a parrot with her." I hear the car in the carport. "I have to go."

Mum comes in the door, and I smell barbequed chicken. I'm famished.

"It's a bribe," she says. "Can you help get Skype on that relic of a computer? Then we can talk to Alex. If you want to."

I just nod. After my shower, we eat in silence while loading up Skype.

If Mum and Lewa ever talk again, it might be to set the terms of a truce.

If Mum and I ever talk normally again, it'll snow in July. But I feel twinges of regret. I sweated out a lot of anger at work today, but she should have told me. I should have known all along about my father. They should have kept in touch. They should have let me see and talk to him. Mum didn't have a computer when I was little, but she could have shown me pictures. But Australia is a long way away and maybe to them felt even farther without the ways to connect we have now. Maybe that was part of their problem.

The computer is too out of date and won't load. What a piece of junk. Between fail four and fail five, I can't help the snort of frustration.

"It's not going to work, is it?" Mum says. She bought the computer almost five years ago with a special Christmas bonus. She sits back and stares at the screen.

I remind myself I'm still mad at her. But she has worked hard for years to give me a normal life. We try again and then give up. I'm relieved in a way. Maybe if I speak with my father, I'd rather he didn't see me. I don't tell Mum about the phone call. I go up to my room to work on my speech.

R. Rigsby

Day 10 Monday: Lewa
Plans and Apologies

In the morning, I call old contacts, not all of them friends of Tropic Watch. Somebody must know why Carlos is so keen to get Piper. One sketchy ex-smuggler, who has long informed me about his former colleagues, tells me the bad eggs using Carlos are ruthless. They're part of a syndicate that sells valuable birds to the highest bidder and the highest bidder in this case is an oil magnate with a taste for exotic pets. Money is no object. The big oil man wants a hyacinth macaw for his collection. One that's tame and friendly.

My ex-smuggler friend says he would never risk giving names to Tropic Watch. The syndicate is powerful and he's afraid of repercussions. But he owes me for an old debt, so he tells me the names of the kingpins. Molecules of ice form in my blood. It's worse than I suspected. Carlos with a few dodgy mates is a nuisance, but these guys are dangerous. I don't want anybody hurt again.

Mitch thinks if I allow Carlos to 'steal' Piper, then I will be safe from his co-thieving friends. He's probably right. If Carlos paid me part of his fee, the money would help a good refuge. Sacrifice Piper for a substantial boost to a sanctuary helping other birds? Then I would be free of Carlos. Alexis and everybody I care about would be safe. Then, if Carlos was smart, he would go back to his village and stay there. Then his mother and sister, who are kind ladies and dependent on him, would be safe too.

But I call Tropic Watch. I explain that Carlos' associates are even worse than I first thought, and I name them. My contact doesn't comment and tells me I should sit tight and await instructions.

Sit tight? I didn't even bring a book. But maybe I should use the time to have a good long think about my life. And whether or not I want a family again, one that includes Alexis. Beth said she gave her the abridged and sanitized version of my history, so she didn't know about my past when I saw her during our interview. But I almost heard the gears meshing.

Then later when I saw her pedalling up the drive, I knew all the possums were loose. Before the end of that long day Alexis knew how I had messed up. Great. Yet, when I saw her yesterday morning, she didn't throw her shovel at me. *Hey kid, don't you know, I'm the family disgrace, and I ruined your life.* Instead, she pointed out a fact that, in my fixation to save Piper, I preferred to overlook.

If I can come up with a plan to deal with that fact, it might help persuade Alexis that I'm not the Mistress of Mayhem. As for Dawn, the animosity between us is like the Great Wall of China. And almost as old. I doubt if an apology will help me scale that wall.

An apology might scrape a toehold in the wall between me and my brother. He used to think my work was a juvenile obsession, like a cult following, and a passing phase. He didn't deserve to have his life bungled either, but I can't rewrite history, as much as I would like to. So, I call Alex. Mother, the only person ever glad to hear from me, gave me his number. I have no idea how to begin.

He answers on the first ring, "Hello?"

"It's Lewa," The weight of guilt flattens all the words I know I should say. I haven't spoken to him since I went to jail.

"Lewa! I hoped you would call."

"Really?" I can't help the nostalgic flutter. My big brother.

The conversation isn't as stilted as I thought it would be. He's awaiting a visa approval. To see Alexis. And Dawn. I tell him about Alexis and how she too has a special connection to birds and, except for being petite and female, she resembles him a lot.

I never get around to apologizing because it doesn't seem necessary, but he says that when we meet, he and I will have a good long chat. That sounds a tad ominous, but still, I'm relieved. It'll be better to say what I need to say face to face. Like when I see my parents. I'll hug my mother and grovel forgiveness at my father's feet.

I apologized to Beth and Nick, who deserve much more. My debt to them can never be repaid. If Nick hadn't spoken on my behalf at my trial, even after all the grief I caused him, I would have received a much stiffer sentence. I told him so while we sat in his shed, watched by his stuffed parrots.

We talked about getting Piper to the sanctuary without fear of ambush by Carlos, or his cronies, which would be worse. We planned our own version of reverse smuggling. He's keeping a check on the quarantine spaces and he's sure there will be one by Saturday. That would be perfect timing, but I have a niggling worry, not helped by Alexis' ingenuous, but true, observation. So far, every effort to place Piper in a good refuge has failed.

I go to the open window in my stale box of a room and look down on a row of dumpsters. Between buildings across the alley, I see a seaplane descending for a landing in the harbour. How would Carlos deliver Piper? I again call my contact at Tropic Watch.

Day 12 Wednesday: Alexis Re-Friending

I ride to the stable in the late afternoon, and the events of this week pass through my mind like scenery along the road. I told Janey all about the Big Revelation on Monday morning. She didn't say a thing. Her eyes got glassy, and she squashed me in a hug.

On Tuesday, Mum and I called him, Alex, after she came in from work–late afternoon for us, but late morning for him. They spoke for a minute and although I heard only one half of the conversation, it sounded like a review of current events. Then Mum gave me the phone and went upstairs.

"Hi," I said, not waiting for him to say something first.

"Why hello, I hear you're working on a school project–a speech on parrots. Are you nervous?"

I was surprised he knew about the speech, but didn't ask and plunged ahead, "Y,yes, I'm afraid I might throw up."

"Ah, yes, it's always hard the first time. But I think you'll find that once you get going, you'll be fine, especially when it's something you care about."

I told him that between Uncle Nick, Lewa, and *Planet and Nature*, I have everything I need, and how I typed and retyped my speech like a mad thing Saturday and Sunday evening. I have enough information to talk for an hour, but I just want to get through five minutes.

After that, we found lots to talk about. He's a marine biologist and does research to protect the Great Barrier Reef! Amazing. An urge to save the planet is strong on that side of the family. If my mother had become a vet, would she work at a wildlife refuge? We didn't talk about Lewa or Mum or anything that happened. Maybe he doodles clocks too.

He asked if he could text or message me to keep in touch, and I had to tell him I don't have a phone.

Gravel spurts from under my tires when I hit the driveway and I'm rattled back to the present. I wish I could ride without my helmet. I would love the wind blowing through my freshly cut, and very short, hair. I went to Snippets right after school and after the cut I thought about dropping by the clinic to show my mother. It's getting harder to stay mad at her, especially after talking to my father yesterday.

I find Cait slugging water in the feed-room on a break between stalls. I pull my helmet off and shake my head.

"Hey that looks great!" she says, but I blunder on.

"Why didn't you tell me about my father?" Minou saunters in and I pick her up. Cait puts down her water bottle and scrubs her hands on her jeans.

"Because I didn't know. I knew Mum had cousins in Australia, but she never talked about them. Neither did Gran and Gramp. Whenever we went to Sydney to see my great aunt and uncle, all anybody said was that this Alexander cousin-guy had a job in Queensland.

And Lewa's name never came up. At least not when I was around."

Minou struggles. I'm holding her too tight, so I put her down. I lean against an open bin and drag my hand through the oats, inhaling the sweet grainy scent. "When did you find out?"

"I found out about Lewa when she drove up in that funny looking van and parked in front of our house. Mum, yeah, people don't tell me everything either, said she had been working back east. Like for fifteen years? I couldn't believe nobody had mentioned her my whole life."

"When did you find out about the bird room?"

"Oh, I always knew the room was there. I think I was in it when I was little. I guess if you noticed it, I would have told you, but I never thought it that interesting. When Lewa asked Mum if she could leave a bird, I stood there thinking, what kind of bird? A turkey, a chicken, a pigeon? As soon as I figured out she meant a parrot, I thought of that carving on the beam."

She tilts her head as if the beam, which is at the other end of the stable, is above our heads. I can't help glancing upwards either. "I always wondered why a parrot was there. Anyway, she told us this bird needed a special place for a short time. She had an apartment in town but couldn't keep it there because she already had her own bird who can be loud enough. You know Piper can be loud? Wow, can she ever. I helped Lewa clean up the room and move Piper in. I knew you would love to see her, but when I said so, everybody jumped all over me and made me promise not to tell you."

"Because they didn't want my mother to find out? And if I met Lewa, she might mention the father I never had? Or Mum might have to tell me the whole story?"

"I wondered why you shouldn't know about Lewa. It made no sense to me. Made no sense at all until I pried every last detail out of my mother last night. That took some doing but Dad, who's back from his tour, said it was time to quit sweeping crap under the carpet. Not quite the words he used, but you know what I mean." Cait swigs from her bottle again. "Such a big deal over something that's ancient history. You should have known all along, but then, I guess they all thought it hopeless. And Lewa is the family girl-gone-bad. Wow! I have a jailbird for a cousin." She chokes on her water. "You have a jailbird for an aunt."

"I thought you knew and didn't tell me. The whole thing seems unreal, even though I talked to my father. He's great, but I'm not sure I want him out here, like it might mean some big changes in my life."

Cait looks up at me. "Some things won't change."

"Still friends?"

"As long as you don't make go near Lewa's birds."

Day 13 Thursday: Alexis
Speaking For the Speechless.

I walk to the podium in the multi-purpose room. I'm first because Miss Gibbs chose to have us appear in alphabetical order by first name. I wish I was named Zelda. The notes in my hand quiver. My hands leave damp blotches.

Yesterday when I got home after talking to Cait, Janey came over and coached me. I spoke, she shook her head. I spoke, she shook her head or nodded, until I read all the way through with no headshaking. She said the video guy is just another person hot to hear about parrots.

Today, it's a 'she' with a GoPro, not a guy. Kendra is a keen You-tuber. Who knew? Maybe we have something else in common after all. She adjusts the aim and smiles at me. Miss Gibbs, with her arms crossed, stands behind the rows of chairs. Faces, faces. All waiting to hear my speech. Rennie and Janey sit in the front row; Janey with her usual huge smile, her legs crossed, and her hands clasped over a knee. She nods at me and in my head, I hear her say 'look up, look up.' So, I look up, and smile.

I clear my throat. My stomach flutters. I take a deep breath. Alex, Dad, said he's still nervous each time he speaks in public, but just starts talking and then it's okay.

"M-m-many of you know I have a pet cockatiel." I stammer, but I think of Piper nickering in her too-small cage. I take a breath. "My bird is just one of many parrot species who live in captivity." I show the pictures of Lola and Piper. "Other parrots like these, are also kept as pets, and not always in ideal conditions."

Then I hit my stride. I explain how difficult it is to give big parrots the space and conditions they need. I tell them about illegal smuggling of birds and how this in contravention of CITES. I tell them that even with increased publicity on the difficulties of keeping parrots in captivity, there are many who ignore the laws and good advice of those who work with these animals. All eyes are on me and even Miss Gibbs has uncrossed her arms and grips the back of the chair in front of her.

"But many people and organizations, like Tropic Watch, work hard to stop smuggling and rehabilitate captive parrots." I don't mention Lewa. I think of her, but all I say is that many people have made personal sacrifices to save birds. "Parrots should not be removed from the wild and the wild places where they live must be protected. Some parrots are dwindling because of loss of habitat, and some are gone forever, like the glaucous macaw."

Loud applause and somebody in the back whistles. Wow! I thought I would puke with relief, but I feel great, so I smile as I take my seat between Janey and Rennie who reaches up and pats my shoulder. Kendra gives me a thumbs up. Aziz is next. He grins at me as he takes the podium. He tells how he first became interested in track and field, and how hard a person has to work to make it to the Olympics. I join in the applause for him and the others who follow. There really is an advantage to going first.

When we get up to go, I tell Janey about my conversation with Cait. "She didn't know anything either, but she agrees that my mother should have told me about my father right from the beginning. I'm still not really talking to her. My mother that is."

I wonder if it's worth the effort. She has apologized and reconnected with Alex. What else can she do? And, I haven't always been honest with her either.

R. Rigsby

Day 15 Saturday: Lewa
A Fork in the Road

Tropic Watch must have erased the big 'X' beside my name, because they waste no time in finding something useful for me to do other than stealing birds. They ask me to pick up a parrot, whose owner has given up. I again call Nick's sanctuary, and the manager says they can take the new bird too because they now have enough quarantine spaces. I can bring the birds any time.

I check out early in the morning and catch a bus to the airport, again going in the departures and out the arrivals, and straight to the parking lot where Mitzi waits, her windows dewy. With tears, I think. In a suburb near the airport, I meet the bird owner also showing tears.

"He's so beautiful," he says, "but I should have done more research. He needs a lot of attention, but I work long hours and often travel on business, so I guess this is best. He's not very tame, but I'll miss him. His name is Chummy."

I understand his pain. He lifts and holds the crate. For a moment I think he has changed his mind, but he shrugs and places the crate in Mitzi. I peek at the bird who sulks on the back perch. I shut the door and off we go.

The morning is fresh, green, and full of good scents when I turn onto the narrow road to my cousin's farm. Neither Mitch nor Maxine have seen suspicious black trucks. They said they would call if they saw anything odd. Expecting Carlos to believe I sneaked Piper to South Carolina was a long shot, but the distraction has bought me the time I need.

Piper and the new bird will have new homes in the sanctuary tonight, but that won't stop Carlos or his associates from stealing and smuggling. And causing the death of more birds. Thanks, Alexis, for pointing that out. I hope Tropic Watch, now that they know who they are dealing with, has a plan. Then Piper will be safe forever and so will everybody I care about.

I don't see the truck until it shoots across the road in front of me from the right. I stomp on the brake. Mitzi stalls. Carlos leaps out and jerks my door open before I can hit the lock. He grabs my arm.

"Let go," I shout in his face, pulling back, but it's no good. He wrenches the keys out of the ignition.

"Enough of this, Lewa, just give me the bird." He slides open the side door and lifts the blanket on the biggest crate.

Blast. I step out onto the ground. Not quite what I had planned. "I don't have Piper. She's in South Carolina."

He sees the boots; his nose twitches. "You didn't take her to South Carolina. That bird is still in the stable. I'm begging you Lewa. Give me the bird. My buyers are sending a plane. I must have her at the airport tonight."

A plane? Just as I thought. Well that might be the solution. But how? My brain ticks over.

"What do you have here?" Carlos pulls the other crate with his fingers in the wire door and then yanks them back with a yip. "Dios mío! You have a piranha?" He shakes his hand. In other times, I would have laughed, he would laughed, but Carlos has changed. He's thin, haggard, and desperate.

"It's a rescue bird. I just picked it up this morning."

"I wondered why you took so long to get here. They told me you left the airport parking lot." His shoulders slump. "I have no interest in this bird, Lewa, just the hyacinth. I need that bird."

"You've spent the money, haven't you?"

He shrugs. "My sister's surgery. If I don't deliver that bird, *I* will need surgery."

"I know. None of us are safe."

His hair hangs in strings. He runs a hand through it. "There's still some money, and I'll share the final payment with you."

"Listen, here's what we'll do."

In the woods around us, robins restart their morning songs, a soft breeze brings the scent of mown hay, and cottonwood fluff drifts along the edge of the road. I resume my drive to the farm, hopeful that by midnight, all my problems will be solved.

R. Rigsby

Day 15 Saturday: Alexis Metamorphosis

I slide out from under the covers but can't slide out from under the fizz in my brain. My speech was uploaded to the school's You-Tube channel and seen by every single person in the school. Didn't anybody do any work on Friday? The roots of my hair warm remembering people asking me about parrots, as if I had transformed into the bird whisperer.

Jas is totally pumped. He wants to kick off the first paper in September with a feature on bird smuggling. Mr. Thoms stopped me in the hall and congratulated me on a great speech. He's sure it will motivate more students to support environmental causes. I thanked him and said I want to do more research. Which I hadn't thought about until I said it.

I let Flip out and she rides on my shoulder and helps me eat my toast. I do my chores: dishes, dusting, and vacuuming. I make my bed and clean Flip's cage. On a roll, I pull laundry out of the dryer and fold jeans and hoodies. A piece of paper drops onto the floor. It looks like a piece of cash register tape. Mum keeps all receipts, and those for groceries go into the grocery tin to check at the end of the month. Or week if it's a tight month. I pick it up. It's a receipt for Flip's seeds, but on the back is scrawled AZ15 and today's date.

Flip squawks as I go out the back door and I feel a pang. I haven't had much time for her this week what with working on my speech and finding out about my father. I have lots to think about while pedalling to the stable. I will visit the birds, then watch Janey ride, and I have talked myself into tackling Mitch.

No black pick-up is parked on the side of the road, but my arms prickle. Why now? I think of the man as I ride by the spot where I dusted the road with my bum. I haven't thought of him since. In fact, I forgot to tell Janey. I have no idea why the man parked his truck there. He could have been, like me, watching birds; I saw his binoculars. He could have been lost and was going to ask directions at the stable. In which case, why didn't he drive up the lane? Or maybe he knew where he was but wanted to stretch his legs. Or maybe I should think about something else.

Lewa's van is parked at the rear door of the stable. She steps out and opens the slider. That would be my *Auntie* Lewa. Two weeks ago, there were a grand total of four people in my family. Now I have a father and grandparents. And Cait and I are suddenly second cousins. Or I guess we always were and didn't know it.

"Bloody Hell."

Lewa, *Auntie* Lewa, needs help. Her arms hug a large crate, slipping sideways. I drop my bike on the ground and run. A bright yellow face pokes above the mesh door. The face's curved beak sinks into Lewa's hand.

"Owww, you little beast!"

"Lewa, let me." Risking a lunch offering to the curved beak, I shove the feathered head inside and hold the door shut. Lewa tips the crate back. The bird thuds to the bottom. It flaps and shrieks, not pleased with the upending.

"There, the hinge pin is on the ground."

I scrabble in the dirt for the pin and shove it back in.

"Bleedin' piece of crap. "Meet Chummy. He's a yellow-headed Amazon and has some bad habits."

"Like eating human flesh?"

Lewa laughs and dabs her bleeding hand with her sleeve. I carry the crate up the stairs, where I learn what that harness contraption is for. We strap the crate on Lewa's back, and I follow her up the ladder and to the loft room. Lewa says he might be named Chummy, but from now on she's going to call the bird Nasty. He is nasty. He squawks and opens his wings, beak open, head down. He tries to bite any body part he can reach.

Lewa mutters a word under her breath, then "That crate is too decrepit to keep him in for long, but he and Piper will be out of here tonight."

"How was the refuge in South Carolina? Is Piper going there? Where did this bird come from?" Too many questions but chatter feels less awkward than a silence filled with too much unspoken.

"Never mind South Carolina. I found something better and much closer. I'm chuffed; Piper will fit in well. This bird," shaking her head at Nasty, "will go there too. I just picked him up from a chap that can't handle him anymore."

Lewa washes her hand at the sink and dabs the oozing cut with ointment. I help her wrap the gauze and look up to see her looking at me. Last week we were acquaintances. Now we are family. We look away. Lewa fills the gap first.

"I love your haircut. How did your speech go?"

"Oh, good. I didn't pass out or throw up, and everybody liked it. Thanks again for talking to me. Lots of kids want to know more about refuges and how to stop smuggling. Teachers too."

Lewa nods. "You might have accomplished as much in one speech as I have in years of tracking down illegal birds." Piper clacks her beak against the cage. Lola fluffs her feathers.

"Hello mate," she says to Chummy, who ignores her.

Lewa looks in Chummy's crate. "You just stay put for a while, Mr. Nasty. Have a chat with Lola. Let's hope some of Piper's Zen rubs off, Grumpy-pants."

I take Piper some banana chips, rubbing her head while she nibbles. Lewa didn't say where the other refuge is located, but I doubt it's in cycling range. I'll miss Piper when she's gone. She really is special.

"Lewa, you didn't tell me where Piper came from. She doesn't have a band."

"She was rescued from a guy crossing the Quebec and Vermont border through rough forest."

"You were there. With Carlos. When you joined Tropic Watch and went on missions."

Lewa stares at me and breathes in slowly. "Yes. The courier picked up the birds, but the smugglers were amateurs. It was far too cold to take birds by foot through the forest. Piper and six other birds had been doped and stuffed into plastic pipes. We had learned which route the courier would take, but he was late.

Delayed by a bridge wash-out we learned later. By the time we seized the birds, only Piper was alive and not by much. We took her to Montreal where an associate had a flat. I stayed through spring break to nurse her. When I left, she went to a refuge nearby."

"Couldn't you bring her back here? There are refuges here aren't there?" Chummy is quiet. Lola and Piper look like they're listening.

"She was still fragile from her ordeal, so it made more sense to place her out there. I hadn't worked with Tropic Watch for long, so I had to go with their decision. But I missed her. She's a survivor." Lewa looks at Piper who lifts a claw and scratches her head.

"I couldn't believe it the day Piper showed up at your uncle's shop when she was supposed to be at that refuge. Some woman who probably thought she looked good with her upholstery said she owned her. Nick knew the bird wasn't banded, but he wasn't buying her, just boarding her for a few days. When I went to work, I recognized her immediately."

"How? If she wasn't banded?"

"How many hyacinth macaws could have the same scar at the corner of the left eye? It's from the sharp edge of a pipe. I tended that wound. When she arrived at Nick's shop, despite everything that happened, she had the most wonderful disposition. She still has."

She turns, hangs a water bottle on Nasty's crate, and sighs. She pokes some food through the door, but he flares his wings and lowers his head. I'm still standing with parts of my face hanging out. "You didn't hear the whole story on why I went to jail. They all think I wanted every bird–"

"But it was just Piper you wanted. Because you rescued her then helped her recover. Then you stole her again."

"I *saved* her again. I overheard Carlos on the phone. He said he had the bird and to bring the cash. His voice shook; he was scared. I couldn't believe my ears. The betrayal: Tropic Watch, me, and Piper too."

Lewa's phone buzzes with a message. She stares at it and frowns. She goes to the window and looks out. Her frown deepens. She lifts her hand to rub her forehead, a gesture I have see a few times, and winces.

"That hand will be sore for days. I can help you, if, that is, if you need help." I get up to look out the window too, but Lewa steps toward me.

"Alexis, you can help me now. I'm taking Piper and Chummy away tonight, and I'm not sure when I'll be back. I look at her hand. "Don't worry, I'll have help, but I don't want to leave Lola here by herself. I'll put her in her travel crate, and you can help me take her downstairs. I'll ask Mitch to take her to my apartment. She can't stay in the house or Cait will sneeze all night."

Day 15 Saturday: Alexis
Roadside Flashback

I carry Lola's green travel crate down the stairs while Lewa hooks the ladder.

"The tack-room for now," she says, and follows me in. She sits on a stool, holding up her hand. Blood oozes through the gauze.

"Maybe you should have that looked at."

"If I do, it won't be until after I deliver the birds."

"Can I go with you? To help?"

She looks at me and smiles, but her expression sobers.

"Not this time. There might be, ah, complications, and I could be very late." Lewa pulls her phone out of her skirt pocket.

I know I look like a little kid who wants to watch cartoons, but Lewa smiles, a little sadly, I think.

"I'm good, if you want to go see your friend now?"

It's Mitch I want to see, so I walk to the end of the aisle. No Mitch. A few horses are in the stable, some are in the paddocks, and some are being ridden in the big hacking field or in the smaller lesson ring, like Janey and Pinball. Most stalls are mucked out and have fresh bedding, but Cait isn't here. I stroll back down the aisle and pat a few noses. I hear Lewa's voice in the tack-room. I don't mean to eavesdrop, but Firefly sees me and leans over her door. I stroke her neck but can almost feel my ears turn toward Lewa's voice. She isn't speaking loudly but grinds out the words.

"...you know the plan. Just go and wait at the plane." Pause. "I said they will go tonight and..."

I don't catch the rest because Lola squawks out "Hello, mate, hello mate," as Mitch enters leading Harley, followed by Brillo. Harley does a tap dance and snorts, but Mitch murmurs to him, and they clop down the aisle together. Firefly gives up on a treat and pulls a mouthful of hay from her manger.

Lewa must now be talking to somebody else. Her voice has a different tone, and all I hear is "Yes, everything is just as I said." This has something to do with moving the birds, which I can't believe should be so complicated. What does a plane have to do with it? Is the refuge farther away than I understood?

I go to Harley's stall. Mitch is bent over with a rear hoof between his knees. He scrapes at a clot of muck with a hoof pick. His hat falls off and his thin hair is even more sparse around the center of his head. Brillo, on guard inside the door, doesn't growl, but lifts a lip to show her teeth. Wow, we are making progress.

"Mitch?"

Mitch lifts his head far enough to take in my old Nikes.

"Yup. What's new, Alexis?"

I take a deep breath. "I've worked here since March, and I think I've done okay?" I don't wait for him to answer. "I'm hoping I can work more hours this summer. I need the money. To save for university." It occurs to me that Mitch too, is a second cousin.

"Ah, yes. Summer." Mitch gently releases Harley's foot and stretches, picking up his hat. Something cracks and he grimaces. "I think we can work that out. Cait wants to take a Spanish course this summer. When she has times and dates, I'll have a better idea what days I'll need you. Will that suit you?"

"Yes, yes, perfect! Any days will be great!" I bounce up and down in my shoes and put my hand up to brush hair out of my face before remembering that it's now cut short.

"And can you bring in the rest of the horses? Maxine and I are off to fetch that lesson pony."

I bring in the three horses left in the paddocks. I would carry them in my arms if Mitch wanted me to. A summer job. I can't believe it. I pat Toady and shut his stall door then run out to find that Janey and Pinball have the ring to themselves. Maxine and Mitch drive by in her pick-up, horse trailer attached.

"Your turn!" Janey slides off Pinball and shortens the stirrups.

"Mitch says I can work here this summer." I mount up.

"Oh, that's great!"

I persuade Pinball to do a few more laps around the ring. Janey sits on the top rail and smiles between pointers.

"You're doing great. Oh, and Royce got his license."

"Well, no kidding. Did you really think he wouldn't pass?"

"No, of course not. And look, here he is!"

The blue Suburban comes to a precise halt facing the ring. Royce gets out, stands beside Janey, and folds his arms on the top rail.

I sit up straighter on Pinball–shoulders back, heels down.

"I can give you a lift home," he says, "your bike too."

They watch while Janey calls instructions or chatters to her brother. I walk Pinball until he's cool. While Janey and I groom Pinball, Royce lumps the saddle and gear to the tack-room. In a few minutes, I hear "Hello mate, hello mate." Royce carries Lola's crate and Lewa follows, rolling my bike with one hand.

"This kind gentleman has offered to drop Lola at my apartment," Lewa says. "You know where I live, right Alexis? The key is under the ceramic frog in the blue flowerpot."

"Yes! We can do that. And this is Janey."

"Hi, nice to finally meet you," Janey laughs, then shuts the stall. We follow Lewa outside where Royce lifts my bike into the back as if it were a toddler's strider bike. Janey hops into the back seat and leaves the front passenger door open for me.

"Do you mind holding her carrier on your lap?" Lewa says. "Lola isn't sure what's going on and you can reassure her. Here's a few banana chips to keep her happy."

Royce has barely reversed and made the turn when I look up from poking banana chips at Lola and see a car rounding the stable: Auntie Beth and Uncle

Nick. It takes me a few seconds to find the button to put the window down, and then I wave and call.

"Hey, what are you guys doing here?!" Another case of mouth in gear before brain engaged. Why shouldn't they be here? They're family friends. Maybe they'll have coffee with Bill and hear about the tour. And of course, Auntie, leaning out her open window, laughs.

"Well, we do get out of our house occasionally, Alexis." What could I possibly say to that? I just give them a thumbs-up as we pass.

Royce stops at the road and looks both ways. I haven't looked ahead at all, because I have a large crate on my lap, and because I keep stealing sideways glances to look at him. I don't see the black pick-up until I see Royce's brow furrow and I look to see what he sees. A man–*the* man–stands beside the truck aiming binoculars toward the stable.

"Hey!" I don't mean to shout.

"What, what!" Royce swings his head right and left then swerves away from the truck.

The man turns his head and looks at us. He sees me. I want to shrink down in my seat, but again hampered by crated bird on my lap.

"It's the man!" I sound like an idiot.

"What man?" Janey and Royce say together.

"The man who knocked me over on my bike. He didn't mean to. I wasn't looking either and I drove into the door. When he opened it."

Royce keeps his eyes on the road, but a muscle jumps in his cheek. Janey, seat belt undone, leans over.

"Alexis," she says, and she never calls me that, "what are you talking about?"

"Sit down and do up your seatbelt," Royce says, "or both of you are walking."

Day 15 Saturday: Alexis
A Date to Remember

Janey laughs when I tell her and Royce about my last meeting with the man in the pick-up. Royce doesn't laugh.

"Have you seen that truck between then and now, or seen the man anywhere else?"

"I think I saw it once in town, but then I don't go around looking for strange men in pick-up trucks." He grins at that, and my spine tingles.

At Lewa's apartment, I find the key and Janey helps me set Lola's carrier on the kitchen table where she can watch out the window. When we come out, Royce leans against the back of the SUV.

"Hurry up," he says, "we gotta go. Dad's taking Mum out to dinner and wants the car. I just saw a black pick-up go by at the end of the alley, but there are probably hundreds in this town."

A shiver goes up my back. I look up and down. A lady with her pull-cart crosses at the street. No truck, no man, no…*Carlos*. Of course. *Duh, Alexis*. I can almost hear puzzle pieces clicking together in my head. Carlos is Lewa's old, what is he? Not a friend, now. He's been watching Lewa. Because she has a valuable bird. Maybe I should go back to the stable.

Royce grins at me. "Jas and I are going to the Snack Shack for pizza–Cait too. Would you like to go?"

But Lewa said she would have help moving the birds tonight. Probably Mitch when he comes back. I smile at Royce. It's not exactly a date, but it's close enough, and hearing Janey in my head (*look up, look up*), I say, "I would love that."

"Ahem," from Janey.

Royce laughs.

"Sure Sis, you can tag along. Let's move. I told Dad I would have the car back half an hour ago."

"Oh," I say, "take my bike out, I'll ride from here; save you some time."

"Sure, we'll meet on the school steps, say in an hour?" I nod and push off.

I ride into the empty carport and chain up. Inside, I pick my favourite jeans from the top of the dryer, glad that I folded them in the morning. The phone rings. Mum says not to worry about starting dinner–we'll order in. I remind myself that I'm still not talking to her, but then, she did call me.

"Oh, Mum," I say, "sounds good but I'm going to the Snack Shack. For pizza or sushi. With Janey and Royce. And Cait. And Jas. We're meeting on the school steps." I can't stop the fifteen years of training, and add, "If that's okay?"

Mum doesn't answer right away.

"Yes. It's okay. I was thinking of pizza too, but you should go with your friends. Take some cash from the grocery tin. And there's a box for you on the coffee table."

Really? There *is* a box on the coffee table–a cell phone box. I rip it open. "Is this mine?" I squeal like a ten-year-old.

"Yes, Alexis, it is. Charged and ready to go."

"But…" is all I stammer.

"Call it an early gift for passing grade nine. And now you can call me, or anybody, anytime." I hear ringing, and barking. "I have to go. I'll call you later."

I can hardly believe it. It's not even second-hand. I dash upstairs with clean jeans in one hand and cool phone in the other. I can't remember when my mother bought herself a new purse. And Auntie is forever chirping that she works too much. But I have worked hard this year, except for math maybe.

Ten minutes later, I'm out of the shower and fishing in my dirty jeans for the money I pulled out of the grocery tin. A key tinkles onto the floor. Lewa's apartment key.

I utter a word I hardly ever use. I didn't put the key back. Janey gave it to me when we walked away. I thought she locked the door, but did she really? Royce asked us to hurry. Drat.

I call Janey and tell her I'll meet them at the Snack Shack, not the school. She's so excited I'm calling on my own phone, that I'm sure she misses the part about putting back Lewa's key.

Envisioning random burglars trying all the apartment doors along the walkway, I peddle in top gear to Lewa's place, and stop at the row of dumpsters. I leave my bike and walk up to Lewa's door. It opens just as I reach for the knob and *the man* and I stand there gaping at each other. *Carlos*. I step back, but he's faster than a striking snake. He grabs the front of my jacket and yanks me inside. Lola's crate is beside him on the floor.

"Well young lady, do come in!" He shuts the door with his foot, catches my arm and twists it behind my back.

"Ow! No!" I yell and squirm.

"No, no, no," shouts Lola. More words I didn't know she had.

"Now, now, young lady, don't yell. I'm sure the neighbours are used to it." He pushes me onto a chair. Lewa's orange scarf is draped over the back. "How convenient," Carlos says as he ties it over my mouth and then ties my hands behind the chair with the long ends. "Now sit still and not a peep while I give your Auntie Lewa a call."

Rage rises behind my eyes. I thrash, rocking the chair, and hmmhmmmm away, but only sound like the vacuum when its clogged. Lola, still excited, squawks, "Hello mate, no, no, no, hello mate."

Day 15 Saturday: Alexis
Gravity Again

I hear Lewa's van pull up in the alley. Carlos opens the door, pulls her inside, and leans against the shut door.

"Alexis! Dear God, what are you doing here?" As if I can answer. I wobble my head around trying to loosen the scarf while wriggling my hands against the knot.

Lewa looks at Carlos. "Let her go."

"Maybe. I might take her along for insurance. So don't do anything stupid Lewa. Did you bring the bird?"

"Birds. You can have them both. Just as we agreed."

Carlos dips his head at the door and yanks me up from the chair. "Then let's get them loaded. You go ahead. And bring Lola. Extra payment for my inconvenience."

I'm not having any of this and strain against the cloth which loosens enough to fall from my mouth. I yell, "No way," and pull back, but Carlos wrenches my arm.

"Shhhh," he hisses in my ear, or bad things will happen to both of you.

"Alexis, do as he says." Lewa's face is white. "You have no idea how this could go."

"Very sensible, Lewa."

I hadn't seen the black pick-up on the other side of the dumpsters. Lewa parked right beside it. She walks ahead of us and puts Lola's crate on the ground, then takes two crates out of the van and quickly places them in the bed of the pick-up.

Carlos drags me by the arm and picks up Lola's crate. I explode with rage and twist away from him, falling against Lewa. My hands are free. Lewa pushes me aside and grabs Lola's crate. She and Carlos play tug-o-war and Lola shouts, "Mi querido, mi querido!"

"No," Lewa says, "Lola is mine. I gave you the others!"

"Come on! Come with me!"

Lewa pulls back but with a vicious yank Carlos pulls the crate out of her hand.

"Your choice," he shouts then lunges forward and shoves Lewa. She falls backwards onto the pavement and cries out.

"Vamos, vamos," Lola squawks.

I launch myself at Carlos. I catch him sideways as he's about to throw Lola's crate into the truck and he drops it hard. Carlos must be part octopus because before I know it, he's holding me in front of him with his arm across my neck. My feet barely touch ground, but I see Royce down the walkway. He sees me too, and quick on the uptake he runs forward in silent purpose. I kick and struggle hoping to keep Carlos distracted.

Lewa gasps and struggles to her knees, cradling an arm.

"Ah, Lewa. Maybe I will take your little niece after all. He tightens the arm across my neck and although I have both hands pulling his arm, he is strong. "You, there, don't come any closer or you'll meet my friend." Carlos releases my arm and reaches in his pocket. Does he have a knife? A gun? Royce, with an expression on his face I have never seen, pauses. I kick but I can barely breathe. Jas, Cait, and Janey run up behind Royce, mouths open.

"Carlos, stop," says Lewa, and pushes the crate forward, "Take Lola, take all the birds, but let her go."

Carlos, maybe realizing that although the entire scenario has taken only seconds, somebody might notice the racket and call the police. He shoves me away from him, grabs the crate and throws it in the cab.

On my knees I gulp air. I'm madder than I have ever been in my life. Nobody has ever manhandled me like that. I bounce up but Carlos' truck roars away. I run after it a few strides with my eyes on the crates in the bed of the truck, Royce right behind me.

"Alexis, are you okay?"

"I'm fine. He can't get away with this!"

Lewa, cradling her arm climbs into the van and turns the ignition. I run up to the door as she crouches in pain, her left arm limp in her lap, and blood oozing through the cut from Chummy.

"Alexis, I have to go after him." She breathes hard, "Can you drive?"

"No, but he can." I point at Royce and climb in.

Lewa vacates the driver's seat and Royce slides up onto the seat and slams the door.

"I've only driven a stick shift a few times."

"No time to worry about that, come on Cait. And you two, get in, if you're coming," Lewa says.

"Oh, boy, I have a bad feeling about this," Cait says but she piles in beside me with a speechless Janey right behind her. Jas with a big grin follows and pulls the slider shut.

"So far, this is way better than pizza!" Then his grin fades. "Are you okay Lex?" To which I nod and then lean over the seat between Lewa and Royce.

Royce shifts. The gears screech.

"My transmission," Lewa screeches. We jerk down the lane toward the main street. My jeans buzz. My phone.

"Mum?!"

"Yes, just checking in to tell you I'll have a surprise for you when you get back." Lewa shouts "Go, go!" which Mum hears, "Where are you and what's going on?"

"Mum, we're with Lewa. We're after Carlos! He stole Lewa's birds. Lewa, where are we going? He's got a huge head start."

"Turn right, go to the highway, and south. I know exactly where he's going. And for Pete's sake step on it."

"Yeah, yeah," Royce says, "But there are lights you know." I'm amazed at how well he handles the Mitsubishi. He glances at me over his shoulder and sees my goggling eyes.

"All last summer at our uncle's farm in Saskatchewan. Drove everything with a motor. Just not from this side."

Gears screech again as we turn onto the main road to the highway.

"Might be a little rusty, though," he grins at me.

I hear Mum calling "Alexis, Alexis!" and look at the phone I'm still holding.

"Where is Lewa is taking you? I can't believe this! Or actually, I can. Make her stop and you get out right now!"

I look at Lewa, hunched in pain, but her eyes blaze. She can't drive and if we stop we'll never see those birds again.

"I'm sorry Mum, we have to do this. It'll be okay, I promise." I end the call and turn off my phone. Janey watches me with wide eyes. Cait grins.

Lewa shouts directions to the highway. Carlos was out of sight before we left the alley, but I stare forward hoping to catch a glimpse, sure that it's hopeless. Poor Piper. She'll spend the rest of her life in a cage. And Chummy and Lola? Carlos will sell them too.

"There!" Lewa points to a turnoff to the regional airport. The Mitz bounces over the speed bumps on the airport road.

"Keep going!" she yells. Royce shifts and steers past the parking lot through an open wire gate and onto the tarmac. He looks at her and raises an eyebrow.

"Well he's not checking in with a load of stolen birds, is he?" Lewa says. "Go, go–they keep the private planes over there–and, yes, yes, there's the ute! I mean the truck!"

Her accent comes on strong with excitement. And yes, I see the truck, and just beyond it, a small plane with propellers turning and its door open.

Before Royce halts the van, I almost wing the door off its hinges, but Lewa is ahead of me running to the plane. Pounding feet follow us.

I see one crate in the open door. Carlos throws in another from which emits, "Ahoy, ahoy, all hands on deck!" Chummy can talk. He's about to throw Lola's green crate upwards. Lewa makes a one-handed grab for the it, but the man shoves her back, hitting her hurt arm. She doubles up. I dodge under Carlos' arm and grab the crate with two hands.

"Why, hello again, young lady," he pants, "Be a good girl and let go, si?"

"Not bloody likely," I gasp back. I've been listening to Lewa. The crate see-saws back and forth, but he's strong and my fingers slip. Wild squawks from the crate. Lola isn't happy with another see-saw ride. My fingers weaken, but Royce reaches over and grabs Carlos' wrist, giving it a twist.

"Just give her the damn bird," he says.

Lola's shrieks of "Hello mate, hello mate," add to the mix while some guy in the plane shouts at Carlos to get in. Carlos wrenches his arm away but shoves the crate. I fall butt first. The plane revs louder and moves away. Carlos runs, catches the door, and hauls himself in as the plane picks up speed. He turns and stands in the doorway, the wind blowing his hair.

"Oh, no…," Cait wails, "He has Piper and Chummy!" She runs forward as if to haul the plane out of the sky, but Lewa pulls her back, and yells something in her ear that I don't catch.

Carlos looks at Lewa, who looks back, an unfamiliar expression on her face as he raises a hand in farewell or invitation, I can't tell. Lewa shakes her head.

Once again Carlos is the cause of my behind denting a piece of pavement, but Janey and Jas help me up.

My stomach sinks. We saved Lola, but Piper and Chummy are gone. I turn to Royce.

"We need to get help, call the police, something!" I whirl and shout at all who seem to be paralyzed, including Lewa. I forget I have a phone in my pocket. I pull it out and turn it on, but Lewa shakes her head at me. She gazes after the plane, tears on her cheeks, and her good arm around Cait's shoulders.

"I think Carlos will be a tch disappointed when he looks inside those crates," she says. I stare at her and remember the mechanical "Ahoy, ahoy…"

"Because he has Uncle Al's stuffed parrots, right?"

R. Rigsby

Day 15 Saturday: Alexis
Pizza and Confessions

Two guys from the airport security run out in time to watch the plane disappear.

"I'm sorry for the confusion, gentlemen," Lewa says, smiling. "My friends had the wrong package," she nods at Lola's crate. They ask Lewa more questions, but since she's hurt, they take her name and number, saying they will follow up. I don't know what the rules are for stealing stuffed birds, but we have Lola, and Piper and Chummy are safe. My phone buzzes in my jeans. Mum. She's probably been calling every ten seconds. I ignore it.

"We better go," I say. Royce is two thoughts ahead of me and has put Lola's crate in the van. I take the front seat and Lewa gets in the sliding door with the others, the van moving when Jas slams the door. Royce doesn't miss a shift and we are soon on the highway.

"Where to now, Alexis?"

"My house." I look around at Lewa.

Eyes that were closed in pain open wide. "Your house?"

"Yes. My mother can check out your arm. And you two need to talk." And I need to talk to my mother. Now. I pull out my phone. She answers on the first buzz. I let her spout for a few seconds and then cut her off, "Mum we are all okay and we are coming home."

I wonder if we've hit a dead zone, but then she says, "I'll be waiting. We'll talk about this later." I'm not sure how much longer I'll have my new phone.

"Can we please pick up something to eat?" Jas says.

"And Mum, can you order pizzas? For seven?"

"Eight," she says.

Cait's eyes run, and she stifles sneezes all the way to our house.

Mum opens the door before Royce halts the Mitz in our drive. I jump down and open the slider. Jas hops out and helps Lewa. Mum comes and stands in front of us. She appears calm, but I feel the rage vibes. I expect steam from her ears.

"You took these kids on this crazy chase, which could have been dangerous for all of them, for a bunch of stuffed birds?" She must have called Uncle Nick.

"Dawn, I'm sorry, he took Lola."

"Once again you jeopardised somebody I love for the sake of a bird. Because of Carlos."

Lewa lifts her chin, but then looks down. "We'll never see Carlos again."

Royce, Janey, and Jas look at each other. Cait looks at Lewa and then at me.

"You guys go in," I say. "Royce, could you put Lola in the laundry room, so Cait can breathe? You two," I look at Mum and Lewa, "make a truce, or something. I don't want to be your excuse for being mad at each other. My life is great. It was before and it's even better now. I haven't had my father in it, but I've had everything else."

My mother stares at me.

"Really Mum, I got a haircut, not a personality transplant."

Her smile is crooked, but she reaches to Lewa. Her expression softens. "Let's go in and I'll take a feel of that arm."

The pizzas arrive and Cait and Janey hand out napkins while Jas opens boxes.

"Oh, man, I could eat the cardboard," he says.

Mum and Lewa join us. Lewa's bitten hand is properly bandaged and her arm rests in a sling.

"I don't think its broken," Mum says, "but have it x-rayed tomorrow."

Between bites of pizza, we hear how Lewa and Uncle Nick made a plan to get the birds to the sanctuary.

"Nick and I had already decided to swap the real birds with the stuffed birds. He would take the real birds to the sanctuary while I loaded the stuffy crates at the back door in plain sight and be a decoy."

"What would you have done if Carlos stopped you and found you only had stuffed birds?" I ask.

Lewa shrugs. "Nick asked me that too, but I didn't care. The priority was to save the real birds and I was sure Carlos wouldn't harm me."

I stare at Lewa. How could she be so sure?

"Then this morning, when Carlos stopped me on the road, I thought of a way to catch Carlos and his mates. I said I would give him Piper to save our families. I would meet him at the plane and Chummy could go as a bonus. Then I saw him watching the stable. He must have been suspicious. I called him again. I said I was sure Tropic Watch was on to us and had alerted the police. I told him to have the plane ready to go. By arriving at the last minute, I hoped to load the crates with the toy birds inside. Then I called Tropic Watch."

"I used a couple of old crates for Piper and Chummy, and their crates for the stuffed birds. When I loaded them, I saw that Carlos was gone, and I thought he had gone to the plane."

"But he believed I had Piper." I put down my pizza. "He followed us to your apartment, but, we, I, forgot to lock the door."

"Locked doors have never stopped Carlos. He called me and said I would never see Lola again if I didn't bring the birds to him. I thought he was bluffing but then I heard Lola."

"He didn't tell you I was there."

She looks at my mother. "Dawn, if I had known, I would have called the police."

Mum opens her mouth, but I look at Royce and the others, and jump in with, "I guess it's a good thing you guys arrived when you did. Carlos didn't have time to look in those crates, and 'ahoy, ahoy, all hands on deck' sounds convincing at first."

"This Carlos." Jas puts down his pizza and looks like he hopes a pen and notepad will arise out of the pile of napkins. "How did you meet him?" Mum and Lewa look at each other. Cait looks at Lewa. Janey and Royce reach for more pizza. I hold my breath.

Lewa doesn't hesitate. "We met in Sydney when I joined Tropic Watch. He was alarmed about the devastation of Central and South American rain forests and the horrible loss of parrot populations. When we came to Vancouver, Maxine's parents let me use the room above the stable as a temporary bird room. We rescued a lot of parrots, here and back east, including Piper, who was then placed in a refuge. But within weeks, she was stolen. Nothing pointed to Carlos. A few months later, Piper showed up in Nick's shop. I tried to save her and went to jail for it."

"You went to jail! Just for a parrot?" Jas, who was starving, hasn't finished his first slice, and hasn't taken his eyes off Lewa. I can almost see his ears pitch forward.

Lewa sits up. "Not just any parrot, an astounding magnificent parrot, and I couldn't bear the thought of her treated like an ornament." She looks at her lap for a second, then looks at Mum. "If I had asked Nick, he might have helped Piper." Lewa looks at Jas and Royce and Janey, who are now paying close attention.

"Piper's owner produced papers for her, and there was no proof she was stolen. Carlos, who could have helped identify her, had left on an emergency in his village. Tropic Watch dropped me like a smelly flannel. I didn't hear from Carlos until I got out. He met me at the prison gate with the gift of Lola, and a load of apologies. He confessed that he had accepted money to steal Piper. Money desperately needed for a new well in his village. He said that another parrot rescue agency had acquired Piper and she was in good hands. That was nonsense of course, but I didn't see it. I was so relieved to be free, delighted with Lola, and after being reinstated with Tropic Watch, eager to get back to work."

"Carlos and I didn't always work together, and I didn't know that all along, he was stealing, smuggling, and reselling valuable birds under threat from his accomplices. If you let them get to you once, they have you forever. He was trapped and afraid for his family. When his associates had a buyer who insisted on having a hyacinth macaw, they told Carlos to find one. Or else. I came back early from a rescue and found her in a crate on his kitchen table.

"Why not call Tropic Watch, or the police?" Mum says, but I answer.

"Because Carlos' scary friends were coming. She didn't have time."

"I grabbed Piper's crate, went home for Lola, and headed west. I called the conservatory here in Vancouver and they said they could take Piper, but when I called Carlos, I told him I was taking her to the Montreal refuge. I hoped that would buy me more time. He begged me to bring Piper back, he needed the money, to save his family, he said. By now he could have saved the whole village. And maybe he has."

Lewa looks paler than ever, and my mother says it's time to get everybody home. Royce and Janey twitch. They are way past curfew. "Cait, you and Lewa wait here with Alexis while I take these guys home." She looks at her watch as they all go out the door.

Cait takes leftover pizza to the kitchen. Lewa rests her head on the back of the couch and closes her eyes. I should help Cait, but I lean forward on the hassock. I take Lewa's good hand and squeeze it.

"Alexis." She returns the squeeze and I hold my breath. "You know if it was a choice between you or a bird, I would always choose you? I would never put you in danger."

I breathe again and nod. Lola, from the laundry room squawks. She's probably asking why she's in isolation. On my new phone, I look up 'querido'– Spanish for 'darling.' Hmmmm.

I hear a car and look out the window. It's not my mother's car, it's a cab, and from it steps a tall man.

R. Rigsby

Day 15 Saturday: Lewa
Timely Arrival

I know who has arrived as soon as I hear the car stop at the curb. Alexis leaves the hassock, opens the front door and goes out. I sit up on the couch and stare through the window. Like looking at a movie on a screen, I see them meet for the first time. Alex, so tall, looking fit and strong, as he should look, from all that scuba diving or whatever he does to count corals on the reefs.

Alexis, not hesitant at all, stands up straight, walks toward him, and then stops. He stops too, and there they wait about two meters apart, not yet ready to move into each other's space. I can't hear what they say, but Alex drops his bag and the backpack hanging from his arm. Anybody else would wonder at how relaxed he looks, but I see tension in his shoulders. He holds out a hand at the same time Alexis reaches out to him. Cait shows up beside me and Dawn drives into her carport. Both Alex and Alexis walk to meet her and out of our line of vision.

"Wow. A family reunion," Cait says. "Did you know he was coming?"

"Yes. But I didn't know he would come here."

"You thought he would go to the farm first, didn't you?"

R. Rigsby

Day 15 Saturday: Alexis
Better Late Than Never

After a night of chasing a criminal bird smuggler and then waving goodbye to a plane load of stuffed birds, I don't expect to meet my father for the first time on our front walk. I know who he is as soon as I see him get out of the cab. At first, I want to run. Hide under my bed. Silly. Instead, I go outside and wait for him to take his bag from the cab driver. He walks toward me.

"Hi," I say, "Well it's not quite here yet, but Happy Father's Day!"

He grins, "It's the best one ever."

I put out my hand and he does too, and then Mum drives up and we go to meet her.

"Hi," Alex and I say at the same time as she gets out, and as if it's the funniest thing in the world, we all laugh.

"Sorry I'm late," he says, then because we all look goofy, "by over fifteen years." He doesn't smile but I do.

"Well you're here now," Mum and I say together, and of course this is hilarious too.

"Let's go in, shall we?" she says. So formal. "I think we saved you some pizza."

I run for Alex's bag and backpack and follow them in the door. Cait bubbles and babbles to her newfound cousin, who pats her arm then turns to Lewa, giving her a careful hug.

"What happened to you?" he asks.

I tell him. Like Mum, he shakes his head at Lewa.

"It's okay." I've never used that tone with adults. But they can be so anal. "We're all fine and the birds are saved. You and Lewa need to talk. That is, I want you to talk. Please?"

They look at each other and at Mum.

"Alexis is right," she says. Then to me, "We will. All of us."

Cait, who hasn't taken her eyes off Alex, looks at me as if aliens just dropped me in the living room.

Later, Alex drives off with Cait and Lewa in her van. He will take Lewa and Lola to Uncle Nick's, then he and Cait will go to Maxine's.

Mum and I sit on the couch with our feet up facing each other, and Flip walks up and down on the back cushions. Flip says more than we do, but it's okay. I'm not mad at my mother anymore, but it will never again be just us.

* * *

The next day, Alex, Dad, comes for breakfast. A Father's Day breakfast. Mum makes waffles and Dad makes mimosas of orange juice and ginger ale. He insists on toasting everything we can think of: maple syrup, the waffle that burns, the smoke detector, and Flip, who we quickly move, until Mum and I sputter in our drinks. He drives me to the stable and helps with the stalls. When he was a kid, he worked at a stable outside of Sydney. Working with my father isn't as weird as I thought it would be.

He says he stayed up late with Mitch, Cait, Maxine, and Bill. He gave them the 'debrief,' as he calls it. He laughs saying it's a good thing the jetlag hasn't caught up with him yet. We're alone in the stable. Janey and Royce are with their dad, as is Cait with Bill.

Afterward, we go to see Auntie Beth and Uncle Nick for the official Father's Day dinner. Auntie heaps food on Dad's plate and chirps that just because he swims with the eels doesn't mean he should look like one. Uncle Nick looks from him to me, and from me to him, as if we have food on our faces. I've never seen my mother blush. Maxine and Lewa join us for dessert after a visit to the hospital where Lewa had her arm x-rayed.

"It's not broken, and it's nothing that time and rest won't fix," Lewa says.

"Mi querido," Lola says from her standing perch. Chummy is in a cage, but Piper too has her own perch.

"What about Carlos?" I put down my forkful of pie.

Lewa reaches over and grips my arm. "Don't worry. I've heard from Tropic Watch. He didn't make it beyond his next stop–Tropic Watch arranged a welcoming committee, and they swooped on most of the smugglers. There are a few stragglers, but the kingpins are going away for a long time. Carlos too is going to jail, not for stealing stuffed birds, but for the capture and illegal sale of others."

R. Rigsby

Day 22 Saturday: Alexis
My New Reality

On Saturday a week later, I ride to the stable early. It's a great way to have thinking time, and I haven't had much of that. Things have a way of happening in ways not expected. Not everything can be predicted, nor can every scheme go as planned. I'm sure Carlos would agree.

Cait's grandparents came home on Monday, and we all had dinner on Wednesday. Unbelievable, a family dinner with twelve people around the table, not just four. Alex, Dad, doesn't go home for over three weeks, so we'll spend a lot more time together. Before he leaves, my grandparents will fly in too. Dad and I Skyped with them on Thursday and my grandmother cried.

I ride up to the gate, and, déjà vu, there's the Mitsubishi at the back door. I look over my shoulder for a black pickup. Nobody is in the stable but guided by some eavesdropping sixth sense that I swear I never had before, I go up to the loft. And hear voices. The ladder is unhooked, and I climb up to the catwalk. And stop. Through the half-open door, I see Lewa wiping the counter with her good hand. The bird room will again be a temporary shelter when the stairs are rebuilt and the doorway re-opened. Lewa is one voice. The other voice, Dad.

"When did you know for sure that Carlos had turned," echoes around the rafters.

"Not until I found Piper in his flat. But I was suspicious before then. I just didn't want to believe it. He would leave but said he was checking on his family. Sometimes he was, but once his mother called me because his sister needed a doctor and she wondered why I thought he was there."

"And Tropic Watch?"

"They knew about Carlos and his underground alliance and had watched him for months. They didn't tell me because they didn't trust me either. I guess that's what love does. Makes you blind."

"Well, you don't think so, but I've always respected your dedication. I–"

For once I don't stay to hear more. I looked through the pictures on my camera and found the one I took in the walkway. Beyond the planter of red geraniums was Carlos, stepping forward, an arm raised. I shivered. I overheard my parents (*I never thought I would ever say that*) talking about Lewa. They hope she meets somebody *not* like Carlos.

Mum will take the afternoon off, and she and Dad will spend the rest of the day together. Mum says she 'is making haste slowly' whatever that means. I don't know how much time she thinks she needs; it's obvious to me. You can't see electricity, but you know it's there.

My father said he and I will see lots of each other, no matter how it goes between them. Before, I would have snarked something like, *so it won't take years before I see you again?* I go back to the tack-room and I'm cleaning Pinball's gear when Dad comes down the stairs. He must have a sixth sense too, because he comes right in.

"Lewa says this belongs to you." He holds out my grubby purple headband. He smiles. "I'm taking Lewa to Nick's then I'll pick up your mother. Last chance if you want to get in on a museum tour."

I shake my head and laugh. "I've been to the museum. Lots. It's free on every third Sunday."

"Rightyo," he says, "We'll pick you up later? You still need to show me the fishing dock and the place with the fantastic fish and chips."

He turns at Lewa's light step on the stairs, and I follow them out to the Mitsubishi. Mitzi has a temperamental moment, but liking Dad's touch, she starts. No gears grind at all. He winks at me and Lewa waves as they chug down the drive. Minou joins me in the doorway and winds around my legs. I watch the van disappear behind trees down the road.

I'm haltering Pinball in the turn-out paddock when, like last week, which seems an eternity ago, the Perrault's Suburban comes up the drive. Royce and Janey. I lead Pinball down the lane and into the stable. He swishes his tail and bobs his head as his hooves clip-clop on ancient planks. This is so normal, so much how things used to be: this terrific old barn, horses, and my friends. A few changes, but inside, I'm the same. Unless I count knowing what I want to do with my life. I will have to work darn hard, especially on math, over the next years to qualify for a good university. Maybe in Australia.

Mitch leans on a shovel in front of a stall, pushes back his cap, and glances my way. I hear a sneeze; Cait's on the job.

"Ah, my two birds," he says, waving at me. Cait steps out beside Mitch, wiping her nose. "Well, Alexis, if you can do four days per week through the summer, you have a job. And Miss Caity here will be fluent in Spanish by August.

Cait rolls her eyes, but then blinks and says, "Yes, Uncle Mitch."

He's not fooled and laughs. I do too.

"For sure, I can do four days every week, or more if you need me." Not one stammer.

"And the next time you guys go on some crazy parrot rescue with my equally crazy cousin, you better take me. I can't believe I missed that. I only get the shovel." He holds it out.

"Funny," Cait says. "Mitch is going back to tech school this fall. Advanced Basket Weaving. I think that's what Computer Science means."

Mitch laughs again. I don't remember hearing him laugh like that. Pinball and I move on to his stall. Royce appears in the doorway.

"Hey," he says.

"You too." I haven't seen him all week, and Janey went home right after school every day. "Everything okay, now?"

"Well the folks were choked. Me with a new license and possibly ruining my chances of going into a police academy. And we hadn't called to say why we were so late. They were all set to hand out groundings forever, until Kendra came over. She and Janey showed the You-Tube of your speech. Kendra said it was important for kids our age to help save the planet and you were the best example she knew. Then we compromised." He smiles, grey-green eyes sparkling.

"Janey didn't tell me." My mouth hangs open. Kendra said that? And *police academy?*

"I think they're proud of what we did, but being parents, they can't say so. And they're happy for you too."

Everybody is happy. Piper and Chummy are safe with Uncle Nick and will soon go to the sanctuary. Lewa has her family back. *Auntie* Lewa. She's excited about the new sanctuary, but there's still something I need to ask her.

Royce leans against a post and watches me, his head on one side. I return to reality. The rattling and scuffling I hear is Janey in the tack-room. She appears in the aisle lugging saddle and blanket with the bridle clamped in her teeth and her helmet perched on top of her head.

Arms crossed, and one leg bent at the knee, Royce leans toward me, "I meant to say so before; I like your haircut."

"Really? I'm not sure. Not in my face, but I wonder if it doesn't make me look like a boy."

"Uh, believe me, nobody would ever think that."

R. Rigsby

Mid July: Lewa
An Alternate Reality

It's too bad about losing the pirate parrot, it was Nick's favourite, but as he said, well worth the sacrifice. That crazy evening, he had seen Carlos on the road too. Nick feared that Carlos had worked out the plan and might follow him instead of me. Instead of going to the sanctuary, he drove home, with Piper and Chummy crated and under a blanket, as if he and Beth had just dropped in for a visit. Nobody followed.

In the next few days, Nick made progress with Chummy who learned to trust him enough to eat from his hand without taking a finger. Then we took both birds to the sanctuary.

It's delightful. They have wonderful outdoor flights, and the inside areas are heated and airy. They have experienced staff and volunteers, including Nick. Their primary goal, in addition to providing homes for parrots, is education.

And Lola and I are part of that. My main job is speaking to schools, colleges, bird clubs, and meeting with lobbyists to not only aid CITES, but to request support for those agencies helping birds. I have Alexis to thank for that. When Cait showed me the You-Tube video of her speech, I made up my mind to take the job.

Alexis doesn't know it, and I could tell she was nervous, but the girl has a gift.

A gift for bringing people together too. Alex, Dawn, and I talked. Dawn said she has spent too much time thinking of 'what-ifs' instead of 'what-nows,' and hopes we can be friends. Me too. My parents flew out.

Alex told them years ago they had a granddaughter. He said Dad harrumphed in his usual way and in his usual way never let on what he thought. Mum, of course, never stopped urging him to ask Maxine about his daughter. When we went to the airport to meet them, Mum practically ran off the plane. She would have trampled anybody in her way and went straight for Alexis, wrapping her in a hug. Then it was my turn. I think Dad took one look at Alexis and his flinty old heart turned to mush. He hugged me too and it's a good thing he didn't ask for apologies, because I could barely choke out, "Hi, Dad."

When Nick and I took Piper and Chummy to the sanctuary, Piper settled in right away. She ate, she preened, she called. Chummy, who I thought would love the place, was miserable. Two days in, despite toys and lots of activity and attention, he hulked in his cage. After quarantine, he met a few others of his kind and I thought he would be fine. He wasn't. But whenever Nick came near, he screamed and hung off the bars of his cage. We quit pushing water uphill then, and Nick took him home. It's about time he had a real bird instead of those dreadful stuffies.

Mid July: Alexis
And That is That

Lewa picks me up at the stable after work, and we head to the sanctuary. Her own temporary sanctuary with Auntie Beth and Uncle Nick has become permanent. I used to be number one in their world, but that's childish. Lewa and Uncle Nick have so much in common, Auntie Beth again has somebody to fuss over, and Lola too has Chummy to talk to if they are left alone.

Mum and I will go to Sydney before school starts. Dad will go back later this week and I have a feeling there will be an announcement before then. No kidding. When he got up to get coffee, I peeked at a website he had up on his laptop: a university here needs a professor for their marine biology program. Lewa plans to go home for a visit, but not until Christmas.

Mitzi hums along the shady roads and both of us watch for hawks on the posts. I keep opening my mouth, but, no words.

"What's on your mind, Lex? You look worried."

Lewa can always tell. "It's Flip. Maybe I should take her to the sanctuary. So she can be with the other cockatiels. She's with Mum today but is often alone. Or I could ask Uncle Nick to take her."

"That's two possibilities. But you would miss her. Who else can help with your homework?" Lewa laughs.

I told her the story about Flip pooping on my algebra, and how I knew then that she had a bird in the stable. "Why don't we see if there's a good candidate to adopt as a friend for her?" She looks at me. "Don't ever play poker. There's more isn't there?" She smiles that quirky smile. "Don't even play Old Maid."

"Carlos."

Lewa looks straight down the road, then at me.

"No. I lied to him. I wasn't even tempted to go with him and take the birds."

Epilogue

It's her first day in the open-air flight. The wire mesh stretches away overhead and farther away it encloses several small trees.

The light voiced human carried her in here just as the sun reached its height. She stepped out of the crate onto the human's arm, enjoyed a scratch, and then climbed onto a branch. The branch is wedged into the corner of the flight, and she wasted no time in scrambling up to a comfortable place with a good view.

She shakes and resettles her feathers. Over several sunrises and sunsets, she became used to the various sounds in this place. Calls and squawks of birds of all kinds, some familiar, some unknown. One in particular caught her attention. From her quarantine cage, she couldn't see the owner of that call, but something deep inside fluttered and made her preen and re-preen already gleaming feathers.

She opens her wings, delighting in being able to stretch them full out, and flaps and flaps. She hasn't had any opportunity to fly for a long time but feels sure she can make it to that lower branch only a few feet away. She scans the area around her and spots a bright blue bird at the other end of the flight next to hers.

The bird has been watching her too. An enquiring squawk is directed to her, and before she can answer, the bright blue bird lifts off and glides to the wire mesh between them. He is gorgeous, but she reaches back and pulls a long tail feather through her beak. She feels no need to be impressed so soon.

Acknowledgements

The birds came to me in a dream and stayed in my mind long after I awoke. I have learned to pay attention to dreams like that, so I scribbled notes, then hammered away at my keyboard.

I finished the first draft, which I admit, took a while. Then I shared it, chapter by chapter, with the ever-patient, ever-honest, and ever-respectful members of my writing group. Their critiques guided me through many drafts: chapters added, swathes of writerly indulgences deleted, characters refined, motivations explained, plot-holes filled and tamped, and any number of nit-picking details brought to my attention and questioned. I thank every one of our Pen & Inklings group, past and present, for their critiques.

Likewise, I valued the comments made by my manuscript readers. Conventional wisdom advises authors not to share manuscripts with family. I disagree, especially if the family member with whom you trust a reading has no problem telling you when a passage stinks or needs help. Or is brilliant. Thankyou, Denise. My friend, Laura, also read an early rendition, and I thank her too for many useful notations.

When it was time for Lewa's Birds to meet my editor, Lynne, she pointed out so many areas that needed work that I wondered if this project would ever fly, pun intended. Back to the keyboard with a better understanding of what I wanted this book to say. Thankyou, Lynne. Along with insightful observations and a scrupulous evaluation, you helped me refine the focus.

And about that focus. Thankyou Grant, who even as I write these acknowledgements asks me how the book is coming. Thankyou, my dear for your support, your confidence in me, and for making dinner. Thankyou Nadine for allowing me to use the lovely photo of you and the cockatoo! Serendipitous and prophetic. Many thanks to the rest of my family too, for listening and for nodding in the right places.

Lastly, I am grateful to the kind and dedicated folks at Greyhaven Exotic Bird Sanctuary who have so generously shared their time and knowledge. And I thank the birds who call Greyhaven home. Some of their stories are heartbreaking. If it weren't for organizations like this, many parrots would not have an alternate home when their caregivers face changing conditions.

It has been a long journey since that dream about birds living in the top of a barn–budgies and macaws, cockatoos and greys, all looking over their shoulders and begging for rescue. I hope this story fosters an awareness of the plights of all wild creatures who, if they cannot be free, should surely be given the best conditions and care we as humans can provide. Thankyou.